Praise for *This Ho...*
Are:

"Short, sharp and tender beneath its skin, Stephen Howard's deeply creepy Gothic novella will keep you up long into the night." **Lucy Rose, author of *The Lamb***

"*This House Isn't Haunted But We Are* explores how grief makes us forget about the present, rendering us aimless, half alive wanderers through parents who have lost a child, and a house who doesn't want to be alone as it nears the end of its life. A heartfelt supernatural and cosmic story about three broken individuals struggling to heal and finding comfort in each other." **Ai Jiang, Bram Stoker and Nebula Award-winning author of *Linghun***

"Stephen Howard blends the Weird, the psychological, and the gothic with easy style. *This House Isn't Haunted But We Are* will draw you in, but watch out - there's far more to it than meets the eye." **Ally Wilkes, author of *Where the Dead Wait* and *All the White Spaces***

"There is an unrelenting sense of dread and horror for the entire duration of the story. The plot is unique and clever. I could see this as a very stylish A24 movie." **Sadie Hartmann, *Mother Horror***

"This House Isn't Haunted But We Are is a novella sized bite of grief horror which offers a fresh take on the haunted house trope. " **Catherine McCarthy, author of *Mosaic* and *The House at the End of Lacelean Street***

"A short but punchy story. I absolutely adored this. Told from three perspectives - husband, wife, house - this book weaves the these narratives together seamlessly to craft a wonderful, gripping, emotionally wrenching story. Exceptional book." **Robert Welbourn, author of *Great Romances of the 20th Century***

"A poignant story of grief, loss and isolation that spans the personal to cosmic. Howard deftly navigates this tale of mourning with compassion and heart." **Suzan Palumbo, author of *Countess* and *Skin Thief: Stories***

"A classic haunted house tale reimagined with a clever, modern twist. Rich gothic storytelling and authentic characters make for a deeply engaging and unique read." ***Craig Terlson,*** **author of the *Luke Fischer* novels**

"Take a classic trope, add a dash of cosmic horror and stir in a ton of grief and you have the recipe for this intriguing tale." **Janine Pipe, author of *Sausages: The Making of Dog Soldiers***

This House
Isn't Haunted
But We Are

Stephen Howard

WILD HUNT BOOKS

This House Isn't Haunted But We Are
First published in 2025 by Wild Hunt Books
wildhuntbooks.co.uk

A CIP catalogue record for this title is available from the British Library

Paperback: 978-1-7394580-6-5
Ebook: 978-1-7394580-7-2

Cover Design by Luísa Dias
Edited by Ariell Cacciola
Typeset by Wild Hunt Books

For those who've loved and lost.

HOUSE

YOU ARE CLOGGED UP and cold, have been for some time, but they might be about to change that. There's plenty of fuel beside you. The caretaker is lazy, but she stocked the woodpile recently, tipping you off to the possibility of them, of new people to inhabit you, fill you up with warmth and joy. You hope there might be children as you so dearly love the sound of children's laughter, their smell reminiscent of freshly baked bread. Your single storey is ideal for young children; no stairs to fall down. But the great outdoors surrounds you, rolling moors smelling of grass and earth; room aplenty to run around and play. Yes, you know you're ideal for children.

You have the loft space, though little ones can't reach it, and you find ways to dissuade anyone from entering anyway. But you're especially protective with the little ones, for whom the sight, that is, what the loft holds, would be... *too much.*

There's a wall of grey, rugged stones separating you from the narrow country road. There's a gate carved into it. There's a car turning through the gate.

They're here.

Wind whistles through your loft. Condensation and black mould wriggle in windows like crust in your eyes that you can't blink away. The car pulls into the gravel driveway and crunches to a halt. They get out and you are disappointed to see two adults, no children. The woman has brown skin and long straight hair neatly tied into a ponytail, slender, wearing smart trousers and a turquoise jumper. The man is white and unshaven, wearing jeans and a grey hoodie that hugs him tight around the waist. His footsteps are heavier. You have seen him before recently, but long ago, too, when you were both younger. She is slower to approach, apprehensive, as if she doesn't want to be here. To you, it appears the man senses this too because he's pointing to the surroundings and half-smiling, nodding fervently, then gesturing towards you and talking a lot. Perhaps, he's convincing her that you're worth it. You feel judged, exposed, vulnerable. You have been hurt before. Tenants come and go, unappreciative, listless in their cleaning, lacking pride in their home. You cannot allow your hopes to soar too high.

The couple circle you, all along the man gesticulating and chattering, the woman nodding but her lips are pursed, her eyes uncertain. Something isn't sitting right with you, but you can't place it. Not at first. As they finish their navigation of the grounds, you realise what is missing; they haven't touched each other once since arriving. You might not be the foremost expert on humans, but many have inhabited you and they are always touching each other, sometimes quietly, tenderly, but sometimes loudly, sloppily, and you try to ignore these displays of affection. But this couple keep a distance from each other. Whether conscious of it or not, they are always at arm's length, minimum. You wonder if they're like you, or maybe they're so unlike you that they don't care for any intimacy at all.

You thought humans were all the same; they all need to be loved, just as you do. Sometimes humans need healing, sometimes you do, too. The couple are standing outside your front door. Hovering above are two birds hanging in the sky before making a swift descent. Above, dark clouds approach. You wait for the two people to enter.

SIMON

THE COTTAGE IS EVERYTHING I hoped it would be. Sure, it needs a little TLC, but Aunt Susan told me as much. I'd seen for myself when I had first rocked up with a van full of furniture. Cousin Tom helped unpack while Aunt Susan nattered about her neighbour's money troubles, old gossip that she is. Anyway, she used to rent this place as a holiday let, but there are fewer and fewer ramblers these days and so the place sits dormant, uncared for and unloved. But we have so much to give, Priya and I, especially since Lily...

I can't.

Can't think about Lily.

I thumb my wallet, which is in my jeans pocket, itching to pull out the photo I have of her, but I resist. It's the last photo I ever took of our baby. Kind of helps this feeling she's still with me. She's smiling in the photo, the gap in her front teeth prominent. Her cheeks are flushed as she'd been running around chasing after ducks by the pond. Our favourite walking spot. We'd all loved it. Tossing bread onto the murky pond surface, playing hide-and-seek among the trees, all that fun stuff. But now...

Fuck. Pull it together, Si, pull it together. Don't let Priya see you wavering, not with the way things have been lately. I'm telling her all the ideas I have for this place that'll make it ours as we circle the property, but there's this listless expression on her face, a glassiness to her eyes which usually means she's checked out. She'd rather be back in the city, probably.

I just can't anymore, though. Too many reminders, too much noise.

"I've got the key here somewhere," I say, rifling through various pockets until I hear the jangling and feel the fierce cold of metal. As I yank my hand from my pocket, a tile from the imbricated roof crashes into the gravel. Priya jumps aside, slate debris scattering against her ankles.

"Are you okay?" I mean to take a step towards her, but my foot stops, hovering above the ground just a moment before landing back where it started.

Priya nods. "Let's get inside."

I raise the key and dangle it as if attempting to hypnotise her. "Shall we do it together?"

Priya stares off into the distance. "It's getting cold, Simon."

She's right, of course. The breeze is biting at my cheeks, and the smell of impending rain is on the air. Further off, where Priya still stares, is a clutch of trees. The leaves and branches are swaying like parishioners during their favourite hymn. Shades of yellow and brown signalling autumn. I push the key into the lock and, not without some exertion, twist it and push the door in.

There's a light smell of damp from sheer disuse. The walls are bare as Aunt Susan cleared the place out for us, but our furniture is in thanks to Cousin Tom and me. There are boxes stacked in the hallway and spilling into the lounge. The lounge is to the right, and you pass through there to the kitchen, which looks out into the sparse North Yorkshire moors. To the left is the smaller bedroom, a child's room, really, and the next room along is the master. Straight ahead is the bathroom. Compact and cute. With a good clean and a lick of paint, this will be everything Priya and I need. A real home. No, a family home. We can fix this place; this place can be fixed. I toss her glances as we move through the cottage, but she's opaque, has erected a barrier between us when, once, we were completely in sync. I hope this project can recalibrate us.

PRIYA

THE PLACE STINKS. OUTSIDE, the smell of manure is heavy and laden with rural turgidity. That sense that nothing is happening at all and that's the way people here like it. Eurgh. Inside, it's damp and fuzzy. I can taste the walls from several feet away. Not my sort of cuisine, truth be told.

Simon waves his hands at this and that, talks about a lick of paint here and sanding down the dresser there. All the while he sounds like the depressed voice inside one of those museum headsets that tells you about art or exhibits in a dreary monotone. I tune him out and wander around our new home. In the city, our loft apartment was open plan with smart exposed brick, a bespoke kitchen, and sleek finishes all about. Here, I see mould stuck in the corners of windows because the insulation is so poor. I feel trapped by the small rooms and low ceilings, as if the sheer weight of my guilt is pushing down upon the structure. I want our marriage to work. I do. I want the spark to come back. But Lily is gone, and maybe it's time to accept any concept of *us* is too.

I stray into the bedroom. There's a small square cut-out in the ceiling. Odd, no handle to open it, but it must be a loft space full of heck knows what. The extra storage might prove useful, or maybe it's sturdy enough for a cute home office. There's a dark stain where the ceiling meets the wall, though, which is probably why Simon wants to fix the roof.

The bedroom has a wide window to allow maximum light in. I wipe away the condensation on the window to stare at the same little stretch of forest I'd seen on arrival. A light mist covers the expanse. I blink several times. My brow furrows. There's a little girl standing beside a tree. I think. As quickly as she appears, she's gone. Stepped behind the tree or a product of my imagination? Or the slippery nature of mist? I'm turning into Simon, seeing things that aren't there since Lily died. It can't be anything more, can it? Wonderful. I've been in this *Wuthering Heights* Hell-hole for five minutes and I'm seeing ghosts. Oh, the wildness of the moors represents the wildness of the characters, so it figures I go mad here. I hope I don't start to stink of shit, too.

Simon walks in and stands beside me. His hand hovers, wants to find its way to my shoulder, but it's frozen in midair, transfixed by the sheer horror of physical touch. I'm glad. I don't want him to touch me. Is there anything worse than being touched by someone you don't want near you? He's the haggard, overweight ghost of my husband. But he is my husband. The version I loved is in there somewhere and if this excursion into the wild is what brings him back, then I'll suffer it for him. There's so much to fix about us, though. Did we really need to add a whole damp building to our list of renovations?

His hand gently lands on my lower back. I shudder.

"Aunt Susan has left us a bottle of champagne. Even popped a little bow around it. Housewarming present, I guess."

It'll be the cheap stuff, probably. I go on staring out into the misty moor until Simon drifts away.

HOUSE

THEY ARE SETTLING INTO you slowly. You watch him as he unpacks boxes of cutlery, plates, trinkets, photos, and so forth. With the photos, he hesitates, lingering over several of them while thumbing the corners of the frames as if they might peel back like fruit, revealing some soft core. Soon, he moves onto cleaning. He takes a cloth and spray to your surfaces, your edges, your nooks and crannies, and his insistent scrubbing tickles you. A refreshing change comes over you brought on by this sprucing up.

But the woman doesn't help. She sits in the lounge all day complaining about internet signal and whether it's safe to go running along these country roads. You had a sense of her reluctance from the beginning. You'd expected the slates slipping from the roof to scare her off instantly. She passed your little test. You need commitment.

They are odd, difficult for you to predict. You cannot reconcile it, that they are a couple, when the animosity and fear is seeping into your walls, so strong a feeling as it is. But already you are used to them, enjoying the presence of humans, feeding on that energy they give off. You are *almost* content.

Something doesn't feel right about you. Something...physical. You can't pinpoint it just yet, but some negative aura, some chronic sense of pain, radiates through your body. You try to forget it.

You watch her leave the sofa – which is white leather, completely unsuited to you – and stop in the hallway to stare at a framed photo that he's hung on the wall. In the photo is him, her and another. A child. Their child. So where is she, this child of theirs? You watch as the woman lifts a hand to the photo. She runs a finger along its glass cover. She delicately slides her fingers beneath the frame. And then she rips it from the wall.

He runs round the corner at the noise but stops and seems incapable of saying anything about the scene. She doesn't look at him, steps into the kitchen, and drops the photo into the bin. He's a sturdily built man, but you see him deflate until he's a sad, limp balloon curled up on the floor. She storms off and shuts herself in the bathroom.

You ponder this odd couple. Despite your misgivings, they can be helpful to you, can rejuvenate you in more ways than one, simply by living inside you. You want them to stick around, you want them to *want* to stick around. But what they are doing isn't living. Something is missing.

The child.

She's gone. That must be it.

Perhaps you can help them, too.

SIMON

THE MUSTY SMELL OF old carpet is comforting, somehow. It always smelled this way, even way back when, and reminds me of happy childhood memories chasing Cousin Tom around the place or playing hide and seek. A long time ago. The sharp bristles of the carpet are rough against my cheek and temple, scratch against my beard. It's not the first time I've laid on the floor and not wanted to get up again. My limbs feel limp. How can she want nothing of our baby in this house? Times like this, we're so far apart that there's no chance we can ever reconcile.

I drag myself upwards, fighting the urge to slump back down, until I'm standing. Do I go to Priya? I don't think she wants me to. Maybe ever again.

My legs take me to the door and outside, into the cold, unsteadily guiding me to the woodpile beside the cottage. The façade is open, but a mesh tarpaulin cover sits over it, propped up by tall wooden stakes. It's rough and ready like the landscape. A stepladder leans against the logs.

I hear a giggling sound. The laughter of a little girl. I peer around the piles of logs, then dash around the side of the makeshift wall, spinning around when I hear it again. My heart is hammering inside my chest, threatening to explode. A trick of the wind? But it's still, no breeze to speak of, and this place is remote so there can't be a little girl running around alone.

The giggles are so familiar. I can picture the grinning little mouth and just the brightest eyes.

"Lily?" I whisper.

There's a sound, but from inside the house. Muffled shouting?

Priya.

I slip, bashing my knees on the hard ground. Shoving myself to my feet, I sprint inside. The shouting is louder now, clearer.

"Help! Let me out!"

Straight ahead. The bathroom! I run to the door and try turning the handle, but there's nothing, no give, no movement.

"It's stuck," I cry.

"I fucking know," Priya shouts back. She's frightened, her voice higher than usual. I don't know why as it's only a stiff door that's stuck.

"Stand back," I say, giving myself a few yards of space. I dash at the door shoulder-first. The frame cracks as I power through and the door itself slams against the wall, a shotgun blast to the ears in this confined space. I fall to my knees again and this time my body stings.

Priya is wide-eyed, her hands to her cheeks. "I heard something," she says, looking past me, as if expecting to see someone else standing in the hallway. She shrieks, bringing her hands over her mouth, trying to contain the sound of fear. Still on my knees, I turn over to sit. In the hallway is a small item. An old rag doll. Just like... just like one Lily used to cuddle in her crib. Aunt Susan collected them too, once upon a time, but we cleared them all out, didn't we? There'd been nothing in the hallway as I came in.

"Priya, what did you hear?"

She sobs, sniffles, then says: "Laughter. I heard a little girl's laughter."

I build a fire using the top-down method and it gets going soon enough. The wall in which the fireplace is embedded is grey brick, with a large mirror set into it. Classic oldy-worldy cottage style. These are the touches that convince me this can be the warm family home we need in a way our city centre apartment can never be. I put the kettle on and make us tea. Priya has the rag doll in her hands. She stares at it.

"It's not going to say hello," I joke, hoping to lighten the mood.

She smiles. A little smile, fleeting, even, but a smile all the same. She places the rag doll on the oak coffee table and accepts her hot tea, taking the cup in two hands. "It's cold in here," she says.

I nod but don't reply. It seems warm to me now the fire is going, but I don't want to tick her off, not after the first signs of civility since our arrival.

"Where did it come from?" Priya asks, her eyes falling on the rag doll.

"It must've fallen out of one the boxes when I was unpacking, and I didn't notice." Priya nods but she, like me, doesn't seem fully convinced. Something in her expression and her eyes tells me so, tells me she recognises the doll's significance, too. Like all married couples, we've a keen sense of each other's feelings, where you know the other person so well their skulls are transparent, and the inner workings of their mind are on show.

"Let's keep it," she says to my surprise. Again, I don't want to unsettle this gentler equilibrium. I pick up the rag doll and sit it up on the mantelpiece. It's a harmless enough looking thing, with gingery hair twisted into spikes and wearing a brown cord dress and stripy tights. Its eyes are little black beads, though, which is disconcerting; Lily's doll had that same blank expression. Priya used to joke the eyes were dead like a shark's.

"It looks good there," Priya says.

"Lily would have loved it," I reply.

Silence. And then an intake of breath. There's the rapping of rain against the window; the erstwhile threatened downpour begins. The pitter-patter against the slate tiles of the roof is soothing, charming even, like the clacking of a tap-dancer's shoes.

Priya takes a sip of her tea. She doesn't make eye contact with me. She gulps her drink down and nods. "Maybe, yes."

I sigh with relief, grasp the warmth of my own drink. Unspoken is a desire to ignore the strange things we have heard today. On Priya's part. Whereas I cannot shake the spark of a thought, a question burning in my brain. Is my Lily here?

PRIYA

THERE'S SCRATCHING AND HAMMERING happening above. Shortly after the noises stop, there's the staccato clanging of boots on ladder rungs. Simon marches past the window, carrying a bag of mulch and leaves and whatever else clogs up gutters. This is the Simon of old, the Simon I married. Handy, busy, proactive. If only he'd worked as hard to keep Lily safe...

No. That's unfair. Blame the driver. It's not our fault, not our fault, not our fault.

The bang of a bin slamming shut makes me jump. Simon. Nearly normal Simon. I daren't get ahead of myself, but things might be moving in the right direction. I miss Lily terribly, but if I focus on losing her every day of my life, then it's not a life, and I'll drown under the weight of that loss. For the longest time, Simon has looked likely to go that way, drifting through this world as more an apparition than a whole human being, but there's a sense of renewal about him. What brought it on, I wonder?

I go back to browsing rugs and throws on my phone. There's Pinterest, Instagram, TikTok, pages and pages of ideas. This place needs warming up if we're going to stay here longer term. I'm trying to visualise the place as a home, though it's drastically far removed from what I'm used to, and give this venture a chance. There's a whole cottage chic to play into. Autumnal colours. A few adornments to make the furniture congruous with the surroundings, get Simon to varnish the wooden beams, top up the tired paint, add a few pieces of art to the barren walls, and hey, presto! A half-forgotten dump becomes a vintage rural cosy home.

The life stuff will follow easily enough. We can both work remotely, and I'll be back to it, thankfully, from next week. Simon is still on compassionate leave, but he'll return to work eventually, I'm sure. He needs to. He can't be slothing off at home while I'm earning money. He should be doing more, if anything. And yes, the income from renting out our city apartment is great, and the company managing it require little from us, but Simon needs to work. He needs the purpose work brings.

After scrolling through a bunch of inane pages of influencers lacking all sense of taste, I switch to Maps and try to get the lay of the land. I need a running route that isn't cutting across farmland. Good. The road circles round and works out at a pretty even 5K, which will do. I suppose I just need to avoid sheep and Land Rovers. Fun.

The door clicks open and Simon strolls in huffing and puffing.

"I'm not as fit as I used to be," he says, grinning.

"I'm about to get ready for a run if you want to join me?" I ask as I stand up and toss my phone onto the armchair.

"Actually, I need to head over to Northallerton. There's an issue with the lead work around the chimney and a few slate tiles to replace. I either need advice or a roofer." Simon steps towards the fireplace, stares up at the ceiling, then places a hand against the brick. "Probably why there's that damp stain in the bedroom. Things will only get worse with the rainy season here."

The stain, a rot that seeps in, spreads, ruins. Another thought pops into my head with its mention. "We should check out the loft space soon. Maybe deck it out as a home office or something?"

Simon nods and his cheeks twitch with a pleased smile. "That we can do. For sure."

He grabs the car keys from the mantelpiece, swoops in to peck me on the cheek, then leaves. I raise my hand to the spot he kissed and try to remember the last time he did that so unthinkingly, so naturally. The car engine grumbles into life. Gravel crinkles as he pulls away. A part of me wishes he'd stayed. I try to remember the last time I wished for that.

The wind picks up as I plod along the country lanes. There's no discernible pavement, but the lines of sight are decent and, since a persistent gloom hovers about this area of the world, I've got my high-vis vest on to help alert oncoming vehicles to my presence. Still, the smell of manure lingers, but it's sickliness diminishes with every day we are here. The refreshing smell of dew and grass is fighting back.

My calves are tight. In my ears, Taylor Swift insists I 'shake it off', which seems like a taunt; it's been weeks since I've exercised. Maybe Simon will get back to it, too. We used to love running together and going to the gym. He always insists on stretching every little muscle, *just in case*. Gosh, it's been so long. Our old gym in the city had a little crèche where we could drop Lily while we worked out.

I try to push the memories from my mind. I want to forget her, but I can't or don't want to, not really, and I feel atrocious for thinking such a thing, wherein volatile anger bubbles and bursts. Rinse and repeat. No. Focus on breathing, on each step, try to find that rhythm. The greenery blurs around me. A light drizzle tumbles down, but it's welcome and refreshing, as if I'm a parched, arid acre, a failing crop in dire need of sustenance.

On I run. The lane bends and I lean with it. I keep close to the shrubbery and hedges. Puddles form and my feet are wet. A hot shower awaits me when I get back home.

Home. Have I called it home yet? Unlikely. But Simon is trying to make it so, so I will try, too.

The hot shower rinses off sweat and rainwater, the warmth invigorating my aching muscles. I've left the bathroom door ajar to appease the anxious nagging of my mind. Doors can stick, but can they lock themselves?

I run my hands through my hair and lather in the shampoo, which trickles down my back. Condensation steams up the glass of the shower. The bathroom is modern, with patterned tiles, a spacious shower and a stand-alone bathtub. The only room Simon's Aunt Susan had started to revamp in the place before letting it slide into disuse.

After a glorious age, I flick the shower off and get out, drying myself in the process and then wrapping a towel around my head. The air is thick with heat. There's the sound of bumbling about coming from the kitchen, so Simon must be making dinner. Good. I'm starving. This revitalised version of Simon has me hungry in other ways, too. It's been so long since we were together like that. So long since I've wanted to feel his touch, his breath against my neck…yes, maybe tonight. I can't help but think it might mend the connection between us. Naïve, perhaps, but plausible.

In keeping with that train of thought, I slip on some of my nice black lingerie. Not that I have ugly lingerie, but these are especially sexy. Once upon a time, these were Simon's favourite set. I splash on the floral scent of Chanel No 5 and wander on through to the kitchen. The little dining table in the corner has a gingham cloth over it. Two candles rest in ornate holders and are lit. A bottle of wine is open with two glasses poured. There's an old CD player on the kitchen counter playing smooth jazz. Something that smells like spaghetti bolognese bubbles away on the cooker. Perfect.

I hear the front door open and shut. Through the kitchen doorway, I watch him toss a couple of logs on the fire, which crackles approvingly in response, and wander towards me.

"This looks lovely, eh?" he says, smiling. His cheeks are rouged from the wind and the colour lends him a rugged aura.

"Why don't you dish out?" I say, steepling my fingers and resting my chin upon them.

"Yes, ma'am!" He flashes me a salute and heads over to the cooker. Still wearing his work skivvies, I note, but the effort he's gone to in every other department convinces me to overlook this minor detail.

The wind whistles through the loft space and I wonder how rough things must be out on the moors. We're isolated here. Any rogue hounds roaming these lands? I don't know Sherlock Holmes, sadly, so we'd be in trouble. But it's oddly soothing, the wildness of nature surrounding us. Maybe I can live here. Maybe *we* can.

Simon places a bowl of sumptuous smelling Italian food before me, having already set the cutlery, and eases into his chair.

"Smells delicious, babe," he says, grabbing his wine glass and offering a toast.

I click his glass with mine. "What are we toasting?"

"New beginnings," he replies, his hazel eyes meeting mine.

I didn't think this day would come. He's still broken, I think, but there's a way forward and that's all I need to know.

I resist the urge to devour my food, knowing how easily bolognese flecks can fly from a rogue fork. Simon is less cautious. In between mouthfuls, he explains various roof-related matters and I zone out a little. I let the music wash over me. I didn't even know Simon owned a jazz collection; maybe he picked it up in town for the occasion? Sweet of him, if so. He still remembers what I like. My Simon is in there. I need to give him a chance to re-emerge, not bristle at his touch, nor turn my anger on him.

I take the empty plates away and sit back down. The candle flames flicker between us and I sip from my wine.

"So, what next?" I ask, finger twirling the edge of my glass.

Simon leans back in his chair and sighs. "I could do with a shower, if I'm honest. I'm beat."

"Well, after your shower, maybe you can join me in the bedroom?" I undo the top button of my blouse and flash him my lingerie. I watch his face. It's been a while since we were intimate, so I half-expect confusion. Instead, his eyebrows rise, and his cheeks flush a little.

"I don't know what I did to deserve all this, but it's my lucky night, for sure!" He jumps up from his chair and scoots over to the door before throwing himself against the doorframe in a faux sexy pose. His best Kim Basinger. I laugh. I always love when he's silly.

But something occurs to me, something he said.

"Wait. What do you mean, 'deserve all this'?" I ask.

His face crumples just a little with confusion, his sexy pose melts away. He looks like he thinks he's done something wrong.

"Just, you know. First you cook me dinner and now you want to go to bed with me, if I'm catching your drift. I do catch your drift, right?"

The warmth of the cottage retreats. I am glass, fragile and transparent, with an icy thaw creeping up me. My eyes flash up to the table, the wine, the empty plates.

"Simon, I didn't cook this meal. You made it, right?" I stand up. The touch of the table suddenly burns.

The candle smells like rotten vegetables. The walls seem closer.

He steps towards the table, placing his directly on the back of his chair and leaning forwards. "I didn't make this meal, either."

I step away from him. My eyes slash here and there, checking corners for some alien face creeping around them, looking for something out of place. I feel sick. The food threatens to come back up and the back of my throat stings.

"It's okay, Priya. It's okay. I think I know what's going on here," Simon says, raising his hands, palms up.

"And what is it then?"

He smiles. "It's Lily. It has to be."

I panic. The walls of my mind are closing in, threatening to squish anything good left in there. I run past Simon and into the bedroom, slamming the door behind me. Simon calls my name but in a benign tone, as if he's sorry for some silly prank that got out of hand. He sounds not himself. His pitch is higher, cooing, even. I grab a suitcase to throw clothes into. That's when I hear it: giggling. I freeze. I can't tell where it's coming from. I dart for the chest of drawers and pull one open, ready to grab what I can and leave this strange house ASAP. It's still blowing a gale outside, but I'll cope. The window is all steamed up. I think, for a moment, I'm going to see a face, but there's nothing there.

Nothing at first.

Lines appear in the condensation. I step towards the window, my hand covering my mouth. Distinct lines, as if caused by a slender finger, are writing something. What's doing this? I stare in horror. Slowly, the words form.

DON'T

LEAVE

I scream through my fingers. Hot breath dampens my hand. I can't keep my eyes off the words, their demanding nature, the threat implicit in them. The condensation. It's on the inside of the window. Whoever...whatever wrote the words is inside the house, inside this room with me. I stumble backwards, spill back out into the hallway and right into Simon. I scream again, this time from shock.

"Priya, what's wrong? Is it Lily?" he says, turning me around, his hands on my shoulders.

"Stop saying that!" I shove his arms off me and push past him, only to hear it again. The giggle. Girlish. Cold. Is it her? It can't be, can it? It doesn't sound like her, but it's something, for sure, something out of place.

"You hear it, too?" Simon says. He disappears into the bedroom. His footsteps thud around the room, but I remain in the hallway. A cold draught seeps under the door. A smell of...of milk? Baby milk, even. What the heck is happening? There's a tightness in my chest, my ribs constricting, putting pressure on my internal organs, threatening to pop everything.

I need to get out.

I rush for the front door and turn the handle. It's jammed. I grab the key off the hook, slot it into the keyhole, and turn. Except it doesn't turn. I frantically try to twist it, switch to two hands, heave, throw my full weight into it as if I might break it, but there's nothing. No movement.

"Lily!" Simon shouts. He stomps into the hallway and his eyes look like those of a desperate insomniac, all bloodshot and stretched wide. This night, so promising earlier on, is becoming a nightmare. Simon's newfound zest a sham. He thinks, what? The ghost of our deceased child is haunting a house she never visited in life? A four-year-old ghost cooked spaghetti? That's not how these things work. Not that I'm accepting ghosts exist, only saying they don't haunt unfamiliar territory or do things beyond their comprehension in life. I've seen films and TV shows, read books, so I know the score. Simon does, too.

He storms past and back into the living room where the fire is dwindling. The rag doll sits on the mantelpiece watching the whole show with a smirk on her face, as if she knows what's going on and can't wait to tell us. Giving up on the door – it seems the house doesn't want us to leave – I slide down and sit with my back against the cold wood, knees up, head hanging between them. Nausea scolds the back of my throat, reminding me of those late-night cigarettes Simon and I used to snag from his dad, back when we were teenagers sweet on each other. Ten years ago, probably. Exhaustion washes over me. My nerves and the last twenty minutes have fried me.

I hear Simon cry out from somewhere around the kitchen, wounded animal that he is. I want to support him. I do. But this might be too much. Then there's that writing in the window. Had I imagined it? Already, my brain wants to rationalise it, explain it away, but it can't. As if hearing my thoughts, a little head pokes out from the bedroom. A young girl. She resembles Lily but isn't quite right. Eyes too wide and heavy, cheeks too chubby, and it's not her smile because it's missing her adorable impishness. This isn't Lily, no. An uncanny substitute, pale and translucent. I hear a faint giggle and the girl fades away. The breath is caught in my throat. I want to move but I can't.

Simon slouches through and slumps down into his knees. "I'm sorry," he sobs, reaching out and grasping at my legs. I pull him up towards me and cradle his head. He didn't see the figure, the not-quite-right figure. Something is going on in this house, but it's not what Simon thinks.

HOUSE

You want to reach out to them, to speak to them somehow, to fix things for them as they have fixed things for you. They sit on the floor, collapsed into each other and leaning on you. You aren't sure why things have gone so wrong, but they have. You worry you've lost them. You nearly did, but you control everything here, including the doors. They need to see how homely you are. They need to see. And you need to trust them, not cage them, and turn them against you.

But they cannot go into the loft. That is your one unbreakable rule. You cannot remove the access point now. It would arouse suspicion, scare them away. Foolish of you to forget about it.

You want to fix things, but especially for him. He paints, he hammers, he speaks of a future. And you see how this affects her, too. How her attitude changes over the course of only a few days. She is thinking of the future. You identify this as important, despite your reservations regarding her, If he needs her then you need her. There is a gap in their life and you're trying to fill it back up but perhaps your attempt at contact is ill-conceived. Perhaps you have misread what they want from you, from this new start in life, and are going to leave you.

Eventually, they rise from their position in the hall-way and move to the bedroom. The fire dies long before they move, though. It's pitch-black outside, and the wind is howling. You are cold and feel your age in your bones, in your bricks, in your foundations. Sometimes, before they came to you, you hoped the wind would blow you down. Better to blow away in one violent day than to crumble brick-by-brick over an age. But they give you hope.

They sleep restlessly, tossing and turning. Finally, they settle. They're at the far reaches of the bed, the maximum possible distance between them. You see the size of the task before you, but rather than shrink from this, you resolve to persist with your efforts. This night is a setback. Nothing more.

Morning breaks on the horizon. A bright cold morning. You know this day is crucial to getting things back to how they need to be. If the malaise sets in, it will be difficult to recover. If you can't recover the situation, there'll be no one left to fix you, and you're aware of some deeper problem, something serious, that desperately needs addressing soon. You need a plan.

SIMON

I FLICK THE KETTLE on and move over to the window, rubbing away the condensation with the palm of my hand. A nice morning. I'll break the lawnmower out today and start doing something with the back garden, maybe nip into town and pick up some cheerful flowers to plant. If I crack on with some tasks then I can shake off the exhaustion in my limbs, in my bones.

Priya hasn't said a word since she woke up. She's probably still staring at the bedroom window like she's waiting for it to move or something. She isn't telling me everything about last night. She's holding back. But why? I'm her husband, after all, so we need to be honest with each other. And I'll take the lead on that front.

I toss the teabags into two mugs and heap a spoonful of sugar into each. The kettle crescendos and the switch *clicks* to indicate it's boiled. I pour the water, squeeze the bags, stir, add whole milk, then stir again. Ritualistic.

I carry the brews through to the bedroom and set Priya's on the bedside table, then climb back into bed with my own. My breath clouds before me.

"How long has your aunt had this place?" Priya asks in a quiet voice.

I sip my tea and side-eye her. She stares at the bedroom window, which has water droplets sliding down it, and pulls the duvet up to her neck.

I tilt my head and glance up at the ceiling. "Hmm. She lived here until Uncle Frank died. Then moved into town after that, which was probably twenty years ago. They were here a good while before, so maybe pushing thirty years." I notice Priya startle when I mention Uncle Frank.

"How did he die?" she asks.

"Heart attack." I know where she's going with this and quickly add, "Nothing violent or bizarre."

She nods her head a few times and reaches for her tea. She has bags under her eyes, probably slept poorly. I didn't get much myself. A faint hint of perfume spills out from beneath the sheets.

"Have you always been close to Susan?" She continues to probe and I'm starting to feel like a criminal being interrogated. Such is the odd undercurrent to her

questions. Keep it together, Simon. Last night shook
you both. Be patient.

"On and off. Her and my mum didn't always get on.
Mum always said Susan was great so long as she needed
you for something, then she'd disappear off the map.
But she was usually pretty good to me, so I never saw
things that way." Birds are calling out in the garden.
Must get us a bird feeder. That'll be a nice thing to keep
up with.

Priya turns to me, finally, and in her eyes is something
new, something bleak and fearful. Maybe I'm reading
too much into it, but she looks haunted.

"I'd like to speak with her, if I can? There's something wrong with this house. I don't know what, but
it's wrong, somehow. Whether your cousin is sneaking
in and fucking with us, or whatever, I need answers."

Priya is pleading. This is unprecedented, as far as our
relationship goes. She's so strong, so in control usually.
She has expectations of me, I know, and I try to keep up
and be the man she needs, but the reality is she doesn't
need anyone. She's entirely self-sufficient. I'm the messy
one. But, looking into her eyes, there's a shift. She needs
me now, but I don't know if I can be enough.

I nod. "Okay. Of course."

After we both shower and dress, I grab us a couple of brioches to wolf down and we jump in the car.

The journey is quiet. We meander along country lanes where the bends are sharp and frequent. Pylons and telephone wires disrupt the otherwise peaceful scenery. Birds sit on the wires and gossip as we drive by.

"I don't know about you, but I'm getting used to the smell of manure," I say, hoping to break the tension.

Priya smiles, I think, and I catch it in my peripheral vision.

"Shit!" I slam on the brakes. Tyres screech as they grip road. Priya cries out.

A little boy stands in the middle of the road. He stares right at me. A man in hiking books and waterproofs hops the turnstile beside the road and fishes him up into a bear hug. He holds a hand up in apology. Kid must've gotten away from him.

"Are you okay?" Priya asks. Her hand finds mine, which is gripping the gearstick so tight it could crush it to dust. My knuckles are white as Priya's hand covers them, tries to warm them, bring about some feeling.

I nod, but the warmth of a tear slides down my cheek. It only takes a second for them to slip away. At least, that's what people say. I know it. Priya knows it.

I start the car up and set off again.

Northallerton Town Centre has cobbles up and down the high street, with car parking on the same stretch. There are rows of shops, but also market stalls with vendors selling everything from fruit and vegetables to old video games and DVDs. Above the shops are flats, and side streets, often splintering off through cobbled archways, opening out into residential areas. Aunt Susan and Cousin Tom live in a cosy bungalow a little ways down one of those roads. Priya and I grab a couple of coffees to take with us. Somehow, Susan and Tom are equally terrible brew makers, so we must prepare ourselves.

As we reach the bungalow, sunlight beaming at us, we stop. I'm shocked. Their place has fallen into disrepair. I glance around the road, see the other, perfectly turned-out homes, and turn to Priya.

"Maybe they've been busy?" I say, resting my hand on the paint-chipped gate.

"It's seen better days," Priya adds, reluctantly.

The grass is overgrown and, frankly, anything could be hiding in it. The brick of the garden wall is crumbling, and debris litters the ground. The curtains of the bungalow are drawn and the place, trying not to be too harsh, looks worse-for-wear.

"So, all your aunt's properties are run down?" Priya says, a familiar note of sarcasm in her tone. If there's one thing that riles me about her, it's how judgemental she can be.

"Not everyone can afford upkeep, or physically can't keep the garden tidy," I say.

"Isn't Tom, like, our age?" Priya is eyeing the dirt-smeared van in the driveway.

I don't want to disappear down this particular rabbit-hole. I open the gate and hold it for Priya. She wanders through and we head towards the front door. I ring the bell, but there's no sound. Broken. I knock.

I see her silhouette through the frosted glass of the door. "Who is it?" Aunt Susan barks from inside.

"It's me, Susan. It's Simon. Priya, too."

A rattling suggests a lock being pulled across and the door clicks open. "Should have said you were coming. Inside with you. Tom is at the pub."

Aunt Susan disappears into the kitchen and asks if we want tea, which I decline with a wave of my paper coffee cup. The bungalow is in a similar state of disrepair as the garden. A musty odour of old things and dust thickens the air, makes it hard to breathe. My mum might have called it 'a bit close in here'. There is a pile of old newspapers by the front door, dark patches of water damage along some walls, and an altogether outdated style of décor. Aunt Susan's cat, a big ginger furball, pads out of the kitchen, takes one look at us, hisses, and shoots off through the backdoor cat-flap.

"Make yourselves at home. Not the armchair though. That's mine," Aunt Susan yells from the kitchen.

Priya and I plonk ourselves into a floral-patterned, dust-filled sofa. I didn't stop by the bungalow when I came to check out our prospective new home. It's been years, years that haven't been kind. I always considered Aunt Susan to be house-proud almost to a fault, but I was still a kid when I visited regularly. Long time ago, really.

Aunt Susan reappears with a mug and places a plate of digestive biscuits on the coffee table. I grab one out of politeness, though I can't admit to feeling much hunger.

"Now then, Simon. Settling in alright?" Susan asks, lowering herself into her armchair. A crossword book and pen sit on the arm.

I find myself nodding, though of course it's not true. Priya silently sips at her Starbucks latte. I dread to think what's flashing through her mind.

"Good, good. Repairs going alright? Plenty to keep you busy," Susan says. She leans forward, almost dipping her chin in her tea, which she cradles in her lap.

"It's looking pretty good, eh, Pri? Painting and cleaning inside are done. Gutters and garden are tidy. Got a roofer coming over tomorrow and I'll be fixing up the garden today." I place a hand on Priya's knee and catch her eye. She smiles, then places her drink onto the coffee table. She clears her throat.

"Susan, have you ever had any complaints about the cottage? You know, from renters?" It's Priya leaning forward now.

Almost reflexively, Aunt Susan rocks back in her armchair. She doesn't answer. Instead, she purses her lips and make a show of thinking hard, eyes slashing upwards, then pouting and glancing side-to-side. I don't expect the next words out of her mouth to be the truth, if I'm honest. She sips her tea as the hands of the clock on the wall tick and tick and tick.

"Can't think of anything off the top of my head." Her eyes disappear into her tea.

Priya rolls her eyes at me. I can't help but agree. Susan doesn't even follow-up and ask why Priya is interested. But there are a lot of things she isn't doing; she hasn't even asked how mum is doing. I know they aren't on brilliant terms, but they still chat occasionally. At least, I think they do.

"No stories from locals, or warnings from the people you bought the place from?" Priya pushes, not being one to leave somewhere without the thing she wants. I want to interject and tell her she's tugging at the wrong thread, but it's not the time for that. It will take more than my say-so to convince Priya that Lily is with us. I'll think of something. For now, I'll let her make her enquiries. Certainly, there's something Aunt Susan isn't saying and I'm curious as to what it could be.

Susan does her little deep-thought routine again and then shakes her head, no.

Priya persists. "Has Tom been over to the cottage recently? Or maybe some silly things going on around town? Kids playing pranks? Anything out of the ordinary?"

Susan's brow tightens. Her eyes flit to a glass cabinet in the corner of the room. Framed family photos stare out at us. And there she is, our Lily, giggling while sitting on my shoulders. A lump catches in my throat.

It's my heart. I'm going to vomit my heart. It's going to plop out onto the coffee table.

I jump up and my head goes woozy for a moment, like my brain is floating out at sea. I recover my composure.

"We should be going," I say. "Please do come and visit us, you and Tom. Come see what we're doing with the place."

Priya rises slowly, reluctantly. Aunt Susan looks, by my guess, relieved.

"We'll do that. We will," she replies.

We get to the front door and step out into the chilly air, fresh and biting, an improvement on the closeness of Susan's bungalow.

"Oh, I almost forgot. Thank you for the welcome gift." Susan stands in the doorway and her face crinkles like she's puzzling over that crossword book of hers.

"Welcome gift?" she asks.

"The champagne?" Priya says.

Aunt Susan shakes her head. "Nope, wasn't me. See you soon, anyway."

Priya and I swap a look. Further evidence of strangeness, she's thinking. I want to stop this train of thought but she's a juggernaut when she gets going. No, best to stay out of the way.

We set off back up the road. The houses and bungalows along here are well-kept, generally, with Susan's being the exception. I do wonder how it came to be that way.

"I'm going to get another coffee. I'd like to look up the reviews for the cottage on the holiday rental sites. Maybe someone said something of interest," Priya says, hugging her long coat to her slender figure.

I don't expect anything to come of it, but no harm in indulging her. I guess Tom is behind the champagne, out of character though it is for him to gift anything.

"Sure thing. Sorry to rush us out. I saw a photo of Lily and it caught me off-guard," I say, sighing.

Priya stops us and looks into my eyes. "It's okay," she says.

"You grab a coffee. I want to get some bits for the garden. Meet you at Starbucks in an hour?"

She smiles and offers me her cheek, which I kiss before heading off along the market stalls.

PRIYA

THE HIGH STREET ISN'T as bustling as the city, and the average age is considerably higher, but I can't deny there's a strange charm to the area. The shops are mostly discount outlets or localised chains, family business types. There's a butchers, an ice cream shop, a funeral parlour, bank, a toy shop, video game store, a whole range. Starbucks and Waterstones are the biggest name retailers here. It's a culture shock, for sure. I prefer brands as there's a certain guarantee of quality. No point in denying that I like nice things.

I nip into a newsagents and reappear on the street with a packet of cigarettes and a lighter in my coat pocket. My nerves are fraying. I fish them out and light up. The smell is intoxicating, thick and smoky, same as ever. I browse the market stalls casually while walking up to Starbucks and it's a hodge podge of knick knacks. Not my kind of thing. Finally, I dip into the coffee shop.

I settle into a comfortable chair in the back corner and connect to the wi-fi. A large — or should I say Venti? – cappuccino stands on the table steaming like a Yellowstone geyser. The place is quiet and smells of coffee beans, which is how I like it. Normally, I have a book and read. I like to picture the Parisian salons and the Gertrude Steins of the world, though I admit the philosophising isn't my strong point. I've always been direct and work best in straight lines, which is probably my dad's fault. He is good at numbers and business, as I am, instilling in me a necessary work ethic, despite the things we had. Studying literature at university was my version of rebellion, I suppose, but still he accepted me into the family business fold and helped me gain the experience I needed for my career. I wanted to offer the same guidance and love to Lily. Now, I can't.

I digress.

I open my phone and start by searching the cottage's address, then bring up the relevant pages on each of the major holiday rental sites. Quick and easy. Most of them use a star review or score out of ten, so I filter for the 1-star reviews and the low scores – there's a lot, which tracks given the state of the cottage – and start scanning the comments for anything unusual.

It doesn't take long.

The first one isn't too bad, but something feels off.

Cottage looks lovely on the outside, and those views! Oh my! Sadly, that's where the good stuff ends. Inside is a little rundown and rough around the edges. Doors tend to stick. My husband got stuck in the bathroom for ages! Would not recommend.

That review is dated five years ago. I scroll on.

This cottage appears quaint and perfect for the area. It's a little remote, but the drive to town isn't too bad. However, the furnishings are extremely outdated and not everything seems to work. Strange noises come from the loft, but we couldn't get up there to find a cause.

Well, at least we aren't getting strange noises from the loft. Just everywhere else.

DO NOT STAY HERE! AVOID! I booked this cottage for a girl's night away and it was awful. Everything seemed okay until we started to get the party going. A weird smell filled the whole cottage and the appliances started playing up and freaking out. It was scary and this place is SCARY BAD. Would NEVER go back!!

This review is from eight months ago. I scroll back and forth on the various sites and these weird negative reviews are scattered among the rest. There's no consistent pattern, it seems, although the ratings are progressively worsening as I trawl the more recent ones. But, otherwise, it seems like the cottage has random episodes where things go catastrophically wrong.

I sip my cappuccino, which is the perfect complement to a cigarette, and stare at the mellow canvas artworks adorning the walls. I focus on them as if meditating. Calm. Relax. Think. What do we do? Or, rather, what can I convince Simon to do? If he thinks Lily is haunting the cottage, ridiculous as it sounds, he'll never leave. But certain things are starting to make sense. The slate that fell from the roof. The doors sticking shut. The strange laughter. The writing on the window. This house is trying to scare us away. But why? In the movies, you need to figure out the secret and try to put things right, fix some miscarriage of justice. Like in *The Changeling* when George C. Scott sets those blue eyes on proving that young boy died at the hands of his father.

The bell at the entrance rings and Simon walks in.

"I've got a bunch of stuff for the garden and chucked it all in the boot of the car," he says, giving two thumbs up. He looks genuinely happy about the prospect of pulling out weeds and planting flowers. There's something else to it, but I don't know what. I'll sit back and observe. It seems we're both hatching plans, but our goals differ.

"Let's get back to the cottage then," I say.

SIMON

I SENSE PRIYA IS holding out on me. She asks polite questions about the garden and the roof, even enquiring as to whether I need help with them. She's very much a Hire-Someone-Qualified type of person, so any inclination towards DIY is out-of-character. She's distracting me. But I don't want to push it or cause an argument. Things have been difficult but, somehow, it's the closest we've been for some time, so I indulge her questions. The drive home is peaceful.

Priya decides to take a crack at some work and cosies up on her laptop in front of a freshly set fire. I tackle the roof first. I grab the ladder and the bag with my tools and replacement slate tiles and clamber up. Luckily, the day remains dry. I wouldn't fancy trying this on a wet roof. I inch up the slope of the roof, bag in hand, eyes on where I'm walking, until I'm in place. My feet feel secure, more-so than I might expect. Safely ensconced upon the roof's peak, I can see all around us. Light mists hover over silver-tinged moorland. The trees look barer, though not yet skeletal. A large bird swoops through the mists, no doubt spying some hapless rodent. The mist swallows them whole. Circle of life and all that.

I pull my pry bar from the bag and wedge it in beside the first cracked tile. The tiles are unfixed, meaning it's an easier job for me. If clipped or nailed in place, they'd be fiddly as hell. And the longer I spend on a roof, the higher the chance I take a tumble. Not that it's all that far to the ground on a bungalow, but it's not a distance I fancy taking at high speed. I'll leave that to daredevils and Olympians.

I ease the broken tiles out of place one by one, tossing them down onto the gravel beside the house. Then, I take the replacement tiles and slide them into place using a brick trowel. They click with minimal fuss and, after a thorough inspection, I'm content to say they're solid. The breeze picks up and tickles the back of my neck like the quiet touch of tiny hands. I remember the first time Lily's little fingers gripped my own. The greatest force ever exerted upon me. So long ago now. A lifetime, even. I don't want to forget, but perhaps I should? Or, if a genie offered me the opportunity to have never known Lily at all, would I take it? Does it make me a horrible person for even considering these things? Focus, Simon. Time and a place, as they say. Roof tiles. The job is done. Time for a brew and then it's onto the gardening. A quick glance at the chimney suggests the lead work will need a proper roofer, being beyond my limited powers of handymanship.

I turn back and she's standing there. Inches from my face. A little girl: grey, translucent, familiar. I yell out in shock and feel my foot slip from underneath me, feel the ridges of the slate as my back clatters against the roof. Yellow and grey and green and black mesh together kaleidoscopically as I tumble.

PRIYA

THE FIRE CRACKLES REASSURINGLY as I review some campaign literature. Marketing used to excite me. Now? A mere job. So much shrinks into meaninglessness these days. Maybe if we can create a proper office, that zest for work, for life, even, will return. Work, apparently, is my only success. I'll trawl through local architecture firms later.

There's a muffled yelp from somewhere and then several bumps above. A second later a tremendous thud, its reverberations shooting up through my feet.

I throw my laptop aside and run for the door. I told him to just get a roofer. Strangely, the door is already open, but it's no time to question this because Simon lies flat on his back on the gravel. I rush over to him and kneel down.

"Simon? Simon, can you move?"

He's groaning. He opens his eyes and squints, though seems to look past me, not at me.

"It's her."

I whip my head up and search for whatever it is he's referring to but see only his bag sitting upon the roof.

"You're concussed, you silly man. No, don't get up, I need to call an ambulance," I say, placing a hand on his shoulder and attempting to ease him back onto the gravel. Simon defies my feeble effort and grunts as he hauls himself up onto his elbows.

"You're bleeding." There's a trickle of blood down his neck. "Let me see." The hair is matted a little, but there's no deep laceration.

"Help me get cleaned up, Pri. I'm okay, honest. Just a little shook up." Simon holds out a hand and I help him up slowly. It's like his various limbs all work but can't quite fire in unison, a poorly manoeuvred marionette.

Inside the cottage, I help him sit on the rug before the fire and fetch a jug of warm water and a hand towel. I take the towel, dip it in the water, and dab at the back of his head. Bit by bit, I unmat the hair, rinsing the blood from it. Soon, the water is pinkish. The aroma of iron nauseates me, but I plough on. Returning to the kitchen, I pour the stained water away, fill a glass with cold water, and take some paracetamol from the cupboard.

"Take these, Action Man," I say.

Simon smiles and gulps them down with plenty of water. The fire crackles behind him.

"I need to get back up there. Need to get it fixed," he says.

"Don't be stupid, Simon, or I'll lose my temper," I reply. "You need fixing first. I can't...I can't." I can't finish the sentence: I can't fail again.

"Okay, okay. You're right."

"Let me run you a bubble bath," I say, forcing a smile and rubbing his shoulder. He does a faux exaggerated wince in response.

"Thanks, Pri." Simon gives me two thumbs up, dork that he is, before pinching the bridge of his nose, no doubt a headache rocking his brain.

I start the bath running and throw in gloops of my lavender bath cream. Swirling the water with my hand, bubbles erupt. I light a vanilla-scented candle, too. Steam climbs the tiles, covering them in that thin wet film. I open the top window to let a little air in.

I head back to the lounge to retrieve Simon and leave the water running. He's not there.

"Simon?" I call, poking my head into the kitchen. Empty. I start to worry he's delirious from the head injury and skip through to the bedroom, but he's not there either. Something catches my eye through the window. It's Simon. He's in the back garden and seems to be looking at the roof. He's got that blasted rag doll in his hand.

I head out through the front door and around the house.

"Simon, hun, are you okay?" I ask, glancing about for some reason he might be drawn here. It's cold and I wish I had my coat.

"She was there. So where is she now? Thought maybe the doll would help," he mutters almost to himself. He doesn't appear to notice me.

I put my arm around him and shepherd him back towards the house. "It's freezing. Let's get you indoors. We'll get you that...shit! The bath!"

I usher Simon into the cottage, flinging the front door shut as I run for the bathroom. I nearly skid into the sink on the bathmat. The tap isn't running. The water looks to be at a nice level and, dipping a finger in, seems to be a good temperature too. Did I turn the tap off? I must have, mustn't I?

Simon wanders in. "Thanks, Pri. Looks wonderful." He seems almost to have forgotten he'd been outside moments ago. He disrobes and lowers himself into the bath.

"I'll leave you to it," I mumble, leaving the bathroom and walking back through to the lounge. The rag doll is back on the mantelpiece. Except, now, it's not alone. Two more dolls have joined it, one either side. They're larger, designed to look like adults. Almost as if they're meant to be parents.

I try not to react. I breathe. Inhale. Exhale. The basics. Either Simon is screwing with me, which seems unlikely, or the strange thing in this house is doing strange things. I don't want to be scared away from the house, but I have no strong ties here. I can happily leave.

I hear a faint noise. A light thumping. Staccato. I strain to listen but it fades to nothing quickly. Usually, these things go bump in the night, not in broad daylight.

I glance at the dolls again. Three sets of beady eyes stare back at me with a grim lifelessness, just like that old one of Lily's. I grab all three of them and hesitate, wary someone is watching me. But this little doll family, they're too much a reminder, too obvious a parallel.

Simon can't see them all together, he's already skirting the edge of something I can't see.

"Fuck it."

I toss them into the fire.

HOUSE

You watch as she throws your gifts into the flames. You are trying to provide them the things they are missing in their lives, but each time things become worse. Despite this, they continue to restore you. Yesterday, she took delivery of the new rugs which warm you in the lounge and bedroom. They're thick and soft. You like how they feel.

But they are not enough to save you. You feel it more now, how vitality seeps from you, leaves you weaker. The situation is dire.

You thought he would be happy to see a little girl, happy to have someone to protect, to parent, to advise. Instead, the shock sends him falling. You cushion the landing as best you can, but he is still hurt. This makes you sad. While he mends you, you damage him. This is not your wish.

But he will survive.

You will find better ways to appeal to not just him but both of them

You see the dolls charring and shrivelling in the flames, a family annihilation, as it were. It stirs you momentarily and the woman pays sudden interest to a sound she can hear, hear but not place. You settle yourself down. If a human can hear you, you are over-excited. If they investigate too thoroughly the workings of your flesh, they may find things that will scare them off for good. You hate the thought of that. Even the woman grows on you. You see her edges soften day-by-day. While the moors are torrid and vast, in here is calm and homely. At least it is most of the time.

You consider new ways to communicate with them. Each time you try, they seem apprehensive and fearful, but then surely it is a simple case of misunderstanding? If they only could receive a clear message and be given the time to regard the message in full, then you would open that channel of communication.

So how?

You notice the laptop she uses to work lay discarded on the sofa. It's a complex device, far different to the passageways through which you manifest and manipulate this small world of yours, but you can adapt.

You can only try. There's no harm in trying, as the humans say.

SIMON

THE BRUISES ARE STILL tender and purple. My brain is loose inside my skull. But I'm alive and surprisingly spritely. Also, the roof is fixed. The roofer sorted the lead work around the chimney this morning. He even complimented the slate tiles I'd replaced and kindly retrieved my bag for me. Win win.

Sitting on the bed, I stare out the window and see another bright and clear autumn day. Priya is out running, this being her favourite weather to exercise in. I glance at the little hatch in the ceiling, the one leading to the loft. I really need to take a look up there at some point. Extra storage space is always useful. A dedicated workspace, even better.

Finally, I reach under the bed and pull out a cardboard box. Lily's toys almost spill out of it. She always preferred playing with the box instead of the toy. Kids, eh? You try and give them the world and all they want is something insignificant and cheap. If I'm right, which I think I am, then there's a version of Lily haunting this house. There's no reason she'll be any different, right? If I have her toys out and ready to play with, including this big box, she might reappear and even stay for longer. I do so wish for one last game with her, to play with her and her toys, to read her a little book about dinosaurs or cats. And what if it isn't only one last game? What if we can play every day?

I carry the box into the lounge and open it. A stale smell escapes. Probably the same kind of pluming stench to emerge when an Egyptologist cracks open a sarcophagus. I arrange the stuffed toys into a circle, all ready to sing Kumbaya, my lord, and they're all so still and vacant seeming, crusty even. They're mummified.

I place a couple of books beside me and sit cross-legged, like I'm back in junior school waiting for an assembly. Tougher on the knees than twenty years ago. The additional smell of burnt wood dilutes the cute ambience I'm aiming for. As there's no fire going yet, it's the remains of what burnt yesterday lingering in the fireplace casting off an odour.

Oh gosh. The mantelpiece is vacant. So then...Priya did it? The charred remains of a rag doll are caught between blackened logs. Why? It was just like Lily's old doll. Does Priya even want our baby back? Because that's why I'm doing this, to bring her back to us, to unite us as a family again.

I sit and wait. The silences stretch on.

But then I hear a thumping sound. A gentle tapping. The footsteps of a child? And the sound is gone. I zone in, focus my sense of hearing, but the beat of my heart seems suddenly to be in my ears.

A child's laughter, sharp and high-pitched, comes from the hallway. Tiny fingers, wispy and slender, wriggle around the door's edge. The beat of my heart is no longer in my ears. It's no longer beating at all. Bit by bit, the flimsy figure of a girl, no more than three or four years old, appears in the doorway. Her eyes point down. Demure, overly respectful even. Not the defiant zest of Lily. But she's a ghost. Something caught between this world and the next. It makes sense she's nervous and unsure. I gesture to the toys and smile at her. Slowly, she creeps over to the circle of stuffed animals and places a finger atop a frayed looking elephant. There's a strange, new smell. Milk?

I remind myself to breathe. This feels like trying to capture an elusive animal, wary of it skittering away if I make any wrong or sudden move. Or, remembering my childhood, trying to catch a rare Pokémon. In my stillness, I hear the thumping again. Coming from...the roof, maybe? No. The loft. That oddly liminal space between the two known areas of the cottage. Could there be something up there? As I stare up at the ceiling, the thumping subsides, and my eyes whip down to Lily. She's staring at me, but the moment our eyes connect she averts her gaze. Shy. Coy. The opposite of alive Lily. I need to bring her out of her shell. I reach for a book and, slowly, carefully, open it up to the first page and show it to Lily.

"Shall I read to you?" I ask. There's no meaningful reaction, but there's no obvious objection, so I elect to try.

"There once was a little star that lived up in the sky. It shined bright enough to give hope to those in the dark."

Lily preoccupies herself with her toys, but I can tell she's listening. I haven't read this story for a long, long time. A lump the size of a tennis ball forms in my throat.

"But the star couldn't shine enough all alone. It needed a little help from its star friends."

I try to hold back, but the pressure inside me builds and builds until, finally, I burst into tears. Lily's ghost jumps and runs away, fading as she goes until she's gone.

"Lily!" I splutter. "Please. Come back." I lay my head down on the rug and pull my knees into my chest. My heartbeat isn't in my ears again, it's in my head, it's thumping, thumping, thumping, bouncing a ball against a wall as a sign of insanity type thumping, only faster. Sweat slides down my back and forehead. I can hear a car horn beeping. I can hear the screech of tyres. I can see a car mounting the pavement. I see everything, just as I see it all every night when I close my eyes. I will never unsee it.

PRIYA

I ROUND THE BEND and sprint the last little stretch before passing through the gate, my version of the finish line, and slowing up until stopping. I press end on my running app and assess the results. My quickest run since arriving here. Excellent.

I wander up the gravel driveway and take in the cottage set against the backdrop of the moors, with woods and rolling hills further off. The more I'm here, the more I could see us staying were it not for the strange circumstances. Even the manure is becoming palatable. Something I never thought I'd say.

I slip my mud-caked trainers off by the door and step inside. I hear a moaning, zombie-like in its low, guttural tone. Stepping into the lounge, I see Simon curled up on the rug, surrounded by toys. Toys I haven't seen for the longest time.

A rush of irritation runs through me, an electric current that threatens to burst out of me in the form of some cynical, cruel comment. I swallow and close my eyes a moment. There's that smell of milk again. It's cold in the cottage. I breathe.

Simon groans but doesn't look up. He's lost well within himself. I lower myself to my knees and lean across him, wrapping my arms around him as best I can, awkward though the angle is. I've come to realise a thing or two since we lost Lily. It took a long time. Too long, really. But that's all part of the process. Grief isn't something with a plottable trajectory. It's one step forward, two steps back. It's sideways movement. It's feeling stuck in the mud, regression, defeat, victory. It's a gentle thumping one minute, tremendous crashing knocks and carnage the next. It's a lake with a serene surface, pleasant and placid, then a deluge disturbing every square inch of surface. And it's never-ending.

There's a lot of shame, too, and it doesn't wash off easily. I'm a failure as a parent because there's one basic goal of parenthood and I couldn't do it: keep your child alive. No amount of logical, practical thinking can alter that in the record books. A freak accident. Nothing could be done. Doesn't happen to people like us. Except it does. It did. And, for me, that shame manifests as anger, and there's only one target within reach for that anger to burst out of me. Kind of like a balloon you keep pumping full of gas until, unable to contain it any longer, the balloon bursts. And that gas? It's toxic. Once released, it's pervasive. It covers everything.

So, I want to be better. For Simon, for me. And, yes, for Lily.

With some gentle coaxing, I have Simon on his feet. He seems not to truly see or understand what's happening, but I lead him to the bedroom and help him out of his clothes and into bed. I kiss him on the forehead and leave him to rest. The ceiling stain catches my eye, growing, as it is, like a cancer. We need to cut it out.

I pop the kettle on and organise an Earl Grey jasmine tea. After that, I get the fire going using the top down method that Simon showed me. I'm not sure I've got the knack quite like he has, but it weakly catches then gets going.

I curl up on the sofa with my tea and pull my laptop over. Better check my work emails, I figure, but I want to show Simon the dodgy reviews the cottage has online. Increasingly, this place feels unsuitable for us. The house wants us gone, that's something I'm sure of. Maybe we can rent somewhere similar, but away from here?

I log into my work account and bring up my mailbox. Bunf, as my dad might say. Lots of bunf. And then something odd. I nearly delete it, thinking of all the cyber security courses they make us do, the risks of phishing scams and all that, but this intrigues me too much. And it doesn't quite look like spam emails I get to my personal account, largely because there's no content at all, only a subject:

OPEN NOTEPAD

Can a hacker do some sort of computer gymnastics if I open Notepad? I doubt it. And I know it's different from films, where they whack a bunch of keys and, suddenly, they're in the Pentagon mainframe or they've crashed the New York Stock Exchange. So, screw it. Maybe I'm losing it, or being irresponsible, but with everything going on I'll willingly search for answers in my junk emails.

I open the Notepad app on my laptop and wait. The cursor blinks at me expectantly, as if I should be writing something. I sip my tea. Nothing is happening. What a fool I'm being. Idiot. I'm about to give up when words appear across the blank white page. All capitals.

IT IS A CHILD MISSING. CORRECT?

The burn of nausea, of bubbling stomach acid, flushes my throat. Is this a cruel joke? Some idiot hacker, after all? I want to shut the laptop down immediately, but there's a rage in me and this is where it needs funnelling.

Listen here you little creep. I don't know how you did this but get the fuck out of my computer and go back to your sad little life.

I sit and wait. My fingers are vibrating with nervous energy. The cursor moves again.

NO. I AM HERE. AROUND YOU. WANT TO HELP.

I toss the laptop aside and rush over to the front window. There's no one malingering, no strange car parked up. I dart through to the kitchen to conduct the same search and there's nothing but a grubby garden and roaming countryside. I return to the laptop.

What do you mean?

I don't know why I'm entertaining this further other than because I started this in the first place. Or maybe stubbornness.

WANT YOU TO STAY. BE HAPPY.

I read and reread these words. Is it Susan or Thomas? No, surely not. Neither strike me as being computer literate. Heck, Susan has a Nokia 3310. No, this is something else. Think about all those films or gothic novels. Usually, there's a ghost that's been wronged and they want you to leave, right? But this is different. Whoever this is wants us to stay. Strange. What did my old English literature teacher used to say? The house is a character *in its own right*. The house is a character...oh my.

Are you...the house?

The cursor blinks and blinks. My eye slash here and there, searching for life in these humble surroundings.

YES.

My heart thumps like I've been glugging energy drinks with a reckless abandon. This is insane. I am insane. But this, the house, it makes sense, it fits. I'm sure. How do I respond?

You can't help us the way you have been. We need to move on. You are right, we lost a child. You can't replace her with a cheap imitation.

I hope to get through to it, to the house. Simon will regress if he thinks he can keep Lily around. But it's not Lily, it's a desperate attempt to fill the void with something that feels the same. It will drive him mad. Something else familiar to those haunted house stories: madness.

ONLY WANT TO HELP. NEED HELP.

I close my eyes. There's a tension in my limbs; a heavy stone in my gut. I need to cut this off now. It's not right.

But how can I make this thing understand? It reads so childlike. It wants us to stay, it says.

Please stop. It will only force us to leave.

There. The one thing it doesn't want, right? I stare at the laptop waiting for a response, but nothing comes. I drain my cup of jasmine inflected tea and tentatively place the laptop aside. The conversation is over. Perhaps our troubles are, too. Quite how I can go on living in a house that's alive is something I'll need to reconcile.

HOUSE

You are unsure how to proceed. She is saying they will leave if you carry on, but you know he will be unhappy to not see the little girl you created again. Is there a way to give them both what they want? If you do that, they will both be happy, right?

You are happy to speak with her, though she isn't the one who cares for you as much. She seems unsure of you and your intentions, as if she has been hurt before. Perhaps another house has let her down. If her last home failed to keep her daughter safe, it's natural she is suspicious and even angry. Yes, this makes a lot of sense. She dislikes houses because they represent something negative for her and are not a place in which she feels safe.

But she is still here. She hasn't left to live on the moors, far from the pain associated with a fixed abode.

You watch her set her device down and stand. She wanders through to the kitchen, stares out of the window, organises the mugs on the mug tree beside the kettle, then goes back through to the lounge. She treads carefully and seems to examine various corners of the room. Finally, she walks through to the bedroom and sits on the end of the bed. She places her head in her hands and you want to offer comfort, but you fear any interference will push her further away. She does not want your help, she says. She does not want to help you in return.

But what if you can make her see how useful you are? How helpful you are? Then she will like you. They will both like you.

There must be a way to give everyone what they want. There must be.

SIMON

I WAKE AND IMMEDIATELY smell bacon cooking from the kitchen, its appealing aroma somehow wafting through to the bedroom. I throw the duvet off and the cold of the room gets at my bare skin. When did I undress? No matter. I grab some clothes folded neatly on the dresser and put them on, doing one of those awkward hops as I shove the second sock over my foot.

A wall of heat envelops me as I walk into the lounge. The curtains are closed, a fire is lit, and so are several candles. How long did I sleep? It must be night time.

In the kitchen, Priya is dishing up a fry up for me and scrambled eggs on toast for herself. There's a bottle of Estrella sitting on the table just a few inches from her glass of wine. It's really cosy in here with lights dimmed.

"Sorry," I mumble, smiling nervously.

"Have yourself a drink, Simon. You've nothing to apologise for. This time, I really have made everything for you." Priya swoops in and kisses me, her hand warming the back of my neck. She's not angry with me?

Priya performs the rapid dance that is buttering toast, doling out beans, scrambled eggs, sausages and bacon, fishing cutlery from the drawer, then bringing all of this to our little table. The smell is heavenly.

"Tuck in," she says, nodding at the food.

I hurl myself into the fray like a berserker. The afternoon took a lot out of me and sleep only replenished one element of my body's energies. Now it requires fuel. I devour all before me like an angry god and sink back into my chair. Priya smirks. She's seen me this hungry many a time, after all. I reach for my beer and wash the food down with a long swig.

"Not out of place in some Viking tavern," Priya says, rising from her chair and grabbing both plates.

"Did Vikings have taverns? Seems like they would, but I'm not sure. Don't worry, I'll sort those pots," I say.

Priya slides the dishes into the wash basin. "Let's leave them until morning. Tonight, let's relax."

I nod in agreement. Priya sits back down, and I raise my bottle, to which she responds and clinks it with her wine glass.

I feel heavy. Not simply from the food, but from the weight of the day, from the contact made with Lily. I want to do that again. I want that to be every day. But more, much more.

"Shall we shift to the lounge? I have something to show you," Priya says, rising again from her chair.

I follow her, intrigue swirling in my belly. I don't know whether I should fear mystery.

We get comfortable and Priya grabs her laptop and fires it up, which confuses me more than anything. But her face is calm. She's not nervous, so it can't be too bad.

Priya types a few things, clicks a few things, then turns to me. "So. So."

She hesitates. Shit. This could be bad after all.

"Yes?" I say.

"I thought I'd have a look at the old reviews the cottage had from when your aunt used to rent it out. I think, like me, you thought Susan seemed pretty shifty when we asked her about the cottage history. I didn't like it. Why would she be evasive? Answer: she has something to hide. Are you with me?" Priya fiddles with the corner tassel of the cushion she's resting the laptop on.

"Go on." I think I see where this is going, but I don't want to interrupt or assume too much.

"Well, there are lots of reviews that report strange things happening here. They go back years and, as you see here, the review scores really nosedive recently. I think something unusual has been happening with this house and your aunt already knew about it when she said we could move in. In fact, I'm sure of it."

Priya turns the laptop so my view is clearer. It's true what she's saying. Even at a glance, I pick out descriptions of things going bump in the night, misbehaving pipes and locks, glimpses of otherworldly things. But none of those things are Lily, surely.

"Over-active imaginations, Priya. People see and hear things that aren't there all the time." I turn the laptop back towards her.

"Can we please invite Susan and Tom round, at least? Let me ask them again about the history of this cottage. Something isn't right, but it's..." Priya stops abruptly, like she's seen something out the corner of her eye. I glance about but there's nothing.

"I don't see the point of riling her up, Pri. Yes, we're putting the work into the cottage, but she's still the owner. She's still letting us use it for as long as we want." I grab my beer from the coffee table. Still cold. Smooth. Soothing.

Priya sighs but keeps her composure. Then her brow creases. "Have you seen this?" she says, pointing to something on the screen.

"I don't care what some old rambler thinks is living in the loft, Pri," I say, tiring of this conversation.

"Don't be an arse, Simon. I'm talking about the cottage description. Look."

Reluctantly, I turn the laptop to me and scan the little paragraph. All dull and typical. Until.

Closed for renovations. Reopening in the new year.

My eyes flit from the screen to Priya and back again. Surely not? Perhaps it hasn't been updated yet but will be soon. My heart is in my stomach. It beats near my belly button and causes some nausea.

"Maybe we do need to speak to Aunt Susan. I'll invite them both round," I say.

PRIYA

SIMON DRIVES OFF, GRAVEL crunching beneath the tyres, and I step away from the window. He's going to invite his aunt and cousin for a drink tonight. Why he needs to do it in person, I'm not sure, but he's off on his merry way now. Maybe he needs some air. Maybe he needs a break from this house or from me. That's fine. Everything is hyper accentuated of late, like within these four walls is a kind of hyperbolic dimension. And this latest hiccup may prove far more significant than even the strange reality that is this house and its apparent sentience.

There it is again, that thumping sound. I hotfoot it through to the bedroom and stare at the little square in the ceiling where I could, in theory, clamber into the loft space. It's tempting to fetch the ladder but, given what I know of the house, I'm too afraid to go up there. Some things are best left alone.

Instead, I set about changing into my running gear. Work is quiet and it's nearly lunchtime anyway. I want to care about work as I once did, but a malaise has set in. The disconnection between city life and here might be fuelling it, but there's no doubt the loss of Lily got it going. But forget work, Priya. Forget it. Frankly, the itch for fresh air is tingling, freedom from the oppressive knowledge the walls are watching. Home should be a safe place where you are comfortable, where you can be alone. The truth is I can't go on living here. I need to raise this with Simon, but not in the house. It's not safe.

It's grey and overcast out, with plenty of wind, so I grab my waterproof jacket, too. Simon has his keys, meaning it's unimportant if he gets home before I'm back, but I snag mine to lock up on the way out. You can take the woman out of the city, but you can't take the city out of the woman.

Another thing to think about: I also want to talk to Simon about going back to work. It's been too long and the chance to focus on something beyond these four walls might do him good. Focusing on some apparition the house creates for him is harmful, dragging him backwards in time almost, stalling the grieving process. I wish more than anyone that Lily could be here with us. She really would have loved the endless fields and hills, the roaming animals, the chirping birds. But she's gone and we're not. I'll wait for the right time, though. If Susan and Tom agree to visit, there'll be more than enough to occupy our minds. If they don't want us to stay then that suits me fine, but they'll owe us for the work we've put into the cottage. Then there's the small matter of whether the house will let us leave. We come and go freely because it thinks we're settling in. If it gets wind of any intention to leave permanently...well, packing should be fun.

I throw my waterproof jacket over me, slip my trainers on, hook up my ear buds, set my playlist going, and ready my running app. Time to clear my mind, if only for an hour or so.

SIMON

I PASS PRIYA AS I round the corner. I'm tempted to beep the horn, but figure she'll not appreciate the scare. I feel in a good mood. Aunt Susan and Tom will be stopping by this evening for a drink and we can get all this silly business ironed out. I don't for one second think there's anything untoward going on, though I can't say Priya agrees with me. She's a much more natural cynic than I, so it's no big surprise she doesn't trust Susan. After all, Susan's been evasive in the past.

I park the car and grab the bag of goodies from the passenger seat. It's been a while since we had these bits in the house. I jog over to the house, rain bursting from the dark clouds above. I unlock the door and step inside, quickly kick off my shoes, then wander through to the kitchen. I unpack the items and chuck the carrier bag in the bin.

There's the tinkle of laughter like the tinny sound of high-pitched piano keys. A warm fuzzy feeling fills me up.

I wash out the new bottles and teats before twisting the lid off a lukewarm baby milk bottle and pour it into a freshly clean bottle. I shake the bottle. Not sure why, but it seems the right thing to do. Could be it does something to enzymes or nutrients, I don't know, something chemical and clever.

The intoxicating lilt of a child's laughter sing-songs through from the lounge. The kitchen is cold. The tiled floor is sharp and shocks me with every step. I cross it swiftly. In the lounge, my breath spools before me. Lily is there. She's as flimsy as those cold breaths, could just as soon dissipate and be gone from sight. But she sits on the sofa, waiting. I step toward her then hesitate. Is this milk too baby-ish? Is it inappropriate? No, she'll like it.

I join her on the sofa. No need to test the milk temperature on my arm, being a pre-made bottle. I remember once feeling the stinging burn of too-hot milk. The memory warms me. I cradle my arm and Ghost Lily shuffles over and settles into it, her shape perfectly fitting into the crook. She's there, but I'm struggling to bring myself to look her in the face. I'm not ready. Not yet.

Oddly, there's no cold sensation. Ghosts send shivers through people, don't they? Lily feels neutral to my skin, room temperature, almost as if she isn't there at all.

There's that thumping noise again. It's only light and soon fades to nothing. The whistling of wind through the loft space and the pitter-patter of rain on the roof replaces it, growing louder, accentuating the stifling silence of the house, of this room.

And then she lets out a melodious giggle. The angels themselves could not produce such a heavenly sound. I look Ghost Lily in the face and she's staring at me expectantly. Something looks slightly awry with her face, but I guess ghosts are projecting to us from some other world, maybe, and that gives their features an uncanniness. She's like a poor artist's copy of the Mona Lisa, but I don't care. I pick up the milk and raise it to her thin, smiling mouth.

PRIYA

I BOP ALONG THE country lanes merrily, my fitness being back to something approaching its peak. The air is cold, but that sharpness tastes joyful. The rain washes over my face as a soothing, cleansing rinse. The problems so present in my mind through the morning are far away. I've outrun them.

I found the final corner and sprint the last few hundred yards, gasping as I dip like an Olympic runner at the finish line. But my finish line is a gap in the stone wall. I throw my hands down to my knees and take deep breaths. Greedy, guzzling breaths.

The car sits dormant to my left as I cross the gravel pit of a driveway and twist the door handle. It's stuck. I try to wiggle it, stir it loose, but it's no good. Locked? That's unusual. Simon rarely locks it behind him, not when he's home. Could be he's gone for a walk in the rain. Either way, I pull my key from my pocket and go to shove it into the keyhole when I realise something.

There is no keyhole.

Where the brass should have a keyhole cut through it is whole. Something looks off about it, but I prod it multiple times with the key and there's nothing, no give, no keyhole. My upbeat mood slithers away. I step back and size up the cottage. Nothing else looks awry. I go to the window but the curtains whip across as if drawn frantically, though I see no hands or body acting upon them.

"Simon?" I shout, banging on the glass. Surely he'll hear me?

I wait.

Nothing.

I sprint around to the backdoor, but it's gone. Completely gone. There's only wall, but wall seemingly built of different bricks. A rush job. Cowboys. But, of course, I've been out half an hour, which isn't enough time.

I stand back. The rain dots my face, cooling the hot flush rising inside me.

I cup my hands around my mouth. "This is my house, too! Open up or we will leave you. Do you understand? Let me in or we're done!"

Nothing happens. Not at first. But my words strike a nerve. The newer bricks tumble out of the wall, but as they hit the ground they disintegrate into dust and blow away. The door, the original door, appears in its place. When all the new bricks are gone, I open the door and run in.

The kitchen is empty and cold, but I hear cooing, that familiar vocalisation whose aim is to soothe a child, and an icy hand grips my heart. I daren't move. But I must proceed. I must. I take tentative steps towards the connecting door, which is ajar, and ease it open.

Simon looks up at me, a foolish grin on his face. He shushes me. "She's just drifting off to sleep," he whispers.

In his arms is the wispy figure of a little girl. Momentary confusion threatens to derail me, an urge to join him, place an arm on his shoulder and dote over our little girl. But it's a lie. Everything about it is a lie, and this house is a virus, capable of infecting us with its illusions.

"No!" I scream. I stamp my feet, ball my hands into fists, almost like a tantrum. "Simon, no."

The sudden noise jerks the ethereal figure from his arms. She tumbles to the rug, then looks up at me. She resembles Lily, but cartoonishly so, the features somehow not moving in a human way. She smiles but her eyes remain dull, her cheeks dimple-less. Simon is seeing what he wants to see. The house isn't producing a perfect likeness, but this isn't reality. It's a poor substitute at best.

The little girl runs past me and it's Simon's turn to shout. I spin round and see the girl pass through the kitchen wall and out into the garden.

Simon leaps to his feet and runs past me. No shoes, no jacket, he yanks the door open and disappears.

I follow.

Rain comes down harder still, churning up the grassy surroundings. Simon is already out the garden and halfway across the way towards the clutch of trees where I first glimpsed something strange. He's racing away like a man possessed, but I know he's out of shape. I set off running too, but steadier, aiming to catch him as he fades.

I'm out the garden. It's slippery. A miracle Simon isn't face down in the mud already. He reaches the trees and stops. He's looking around them and, as I close in, I hear he's shouting her name over and over again.

I reach the trees and he's slumped on his knees, bark covering his jeans, his hands grasping at dirt.

"She's gone again. You scared her away," he says, glancing up at me. In the dark cover of this tiny forest, his eyes glint with a madness I only know from gothic literature. But I can't meet him with anger or hatred. Not anymore.

I edge over to him and crouch down. I take his hands in mine, close my eyes, then lean my forehead against his.

"She isn't real, Simon. She isn't our Lily. She isn't her ghost. It's the house. The house is alive and it's trying to give you what it thinks you want. But it's no good for us, Si. She's never coming back. We hurt ourselves every time we think otherwise. I'm so sorry I haven't handled things as I should have. You externalised your pain, but I turned mine inwards. I thought to injure only myself. But instead, I grew cold and weary. I'm so sorry. I'm so sorry." I kiss his forehead, bring him into an embrace. Earthy smells of mud and rain and trees infiltrate my brain. Slowly, steadily, I feel Simon wilt, feel him give in to me and return my hug.

I open my eyes.

Beyond the trees a mist descends. No one stands in the tall grass watching us. We are alone.

HOUSE

You watch them chasing after the little girl, but you can't sustain the form too far beyond your boundaries. She fades away within the trees. He falls to his knees.

The veins of you are clear, your innards clean and efficient in their work, your skin as fresh and vibrant as the countryside air around you. You are close to looking and feeling your absolute best. You are warm and comfortable, you are content. This is all down to them. But the malignancy is in your heart, and it grows each day.

They cannot know that, though. While they are ever proving themselves to you, you are failing them.

Foolish to think keeping them apart, satisfying their needs separately, is possible. Inside you, there is little room for secrecy.

You fix up any other edits to your form, return the keyhole to the front door. You feel the anxiety, the sense that once again you risk losing your best tenants since, well, *them*. The ones who love you always. *Loved* you. You failed them, too.

They are walking slowly across the moors, silhouettes against the thickening mist. As they near, you see they are trembling. Despite your misgivings about further interference, you start up a fire and hope this will be a welcome surprise. As they hobble into the garden they appear almost as one whole being, their sharp edges somehow clicking into each other's nooks and crevices. You remember thinking they are a strange match, seemingly incompatible. But now they are different. Now, they fit together.

But this presents a problem, too.

She remains uncertain. Does he see things as she does? If she leaves, does he leave? If she disappears, does he stay? If he cannot see his little girl again, will he want to go? You seek solutions and yet create further problems. If you speak to her again, can you successfully convince her there is a way forward for you all? If you cannot, what happens then? Maybe there's a way. Maybe.

Or she has to go.

SIMON

THE CHILL IS STILL in my bones. I stand in the shower and try to remember ever feeling warm, feeling happy, but darkness clouds my mind. Steam billows around me. I step out of the shower and towel myself down, trying to shake the heaviness from each limb. I have to face up to something and I don't know how.

The bathroom door clicks open.

"Susan and Tom will be here soon." Priya leans against the door. I see pity in her eyes. I can't decide if it's better or worse than the anger and disdain they held upon our arrival at the cottage. But I forgot about our evening plans.

"Oh, damn. I'll get ready."

"We can cancel if you'd prefer?" Priya asks.

I shake my head, no. "Best to get this over with. We'll sleep tonight, eh?"

Priya smiles. "I'll get a few snacks and drinks ready."

She disappears through to the kitchen. I head through to the bedroom to set about getting dressed. In the top corner, malingering where the ceiling meets the wall above the door, the stain growls. Another thing to fix, but it can wait.

The now familiar sound of tyres on gravel indicates their arrival. Priya meets my eyes and raises her eyebrows as if to say, *here we go*.

I answer the knock at the door and welcome them in. Tom grunts and nods, Susan strolls in without a word. Something about their manner makes me wonder if they suspect something, whether they're expecting an interrogation. I suppress a yawn and follow them through to the lounge.

The fire crackles invitingly, the lamp light throws shadows at odd angles. They sit themselves down on the sofa.

"Wine?" Priya asks.

"Beer, if you've got any," Tom says in his broad, Geoffrey Boycott accent.

"One minute," I respond, rising and nipping through to the kitchen. Tom will be driving home, but I don't expect that to stop him drinking his fill. No doubt he's been in the pub already. I grab two beers from the fridge and return to the silence of the lounge. I place one of the beers on the coffee table for Tom, then retreat to the armchair where Priya is sitting. I perch on the arm, by Priya's side, facing my family, showing solidarity.

The can *tsks* as Tom cracks his open with force. I do mine with considered care.

"The house looks different," Susan says while affecting an exaggerated look around the room. I notice this isn't exactly a compliment, but skate past it.

"We've put a bit of money in. Roof, garden, decorating. Of course, Priya is the expert there. I just do the grunt work." I smile at Priya, who offers one back.

"Wasn't sure a city boy could get his hands dirty." Tom swigs from his can and nudges Aunt Susan, though she doesn't quite join in with his giggling.

That light thumping noise starts up. I can't tell if Tom and Susan hear it at first as they don't seem to stir or startle, but Tom's eyes are soon drawn upwards.

"Squirrels? Can get you some traps if you need them. Gotta get up there though. If one dies it'll be an awful stink. Trust me," he says, with Susan nodding sagely beside him.

"I do keep meaning to explore the loft space. Looks like there's a leak somewhere above the bedroom so I'll check it tomorrow," I respond.

The thumping escalates.

"A squirrel party, it seems," Priya jokes, trying to lighten the mood.

"So, Simon, how are you liking the cottage?" Susan asks out of the blue. She's been oddly reticent so far.

"We both like it very much." I lay a hand on Priya's shoulder.

"Been a good while. Needed doing up, it did. Such a pretty place attracts people. Got those woods over yonder, too." Susan's eyes roam the room again, giving the impression she's speaking almost to herself.

Priya and I swap a glance. Something is definitely awry.

Priya clears her throat. "Did you always rent the cottage as a holiday let?"

I smirk. I'm not sure if Susan or Tom will pick up on it, but I'm sure Priya is still trying to pry information from them about the house's history. She's very persistent.

It's Tom and Susan swapping a glance now.

"No," Aunt Susan says, "not always. Used to be a couple had the place for a good while. Well-to-do couple. Wanted a rural place to raise a family and all that. The sort of city dwellers who think living out this way is like *The Sound of Music* or something." Susan reaches for her wine.

"Did it not work out?" I ask. I don't remember any couple or a family, but it might have been when mum and Susan were on bad terms.

Tom pauses with his can halfway to his mouth. Susan purses her lips, then places her wine glass back on the table.

"They disappeared. Here one day, gone the next. Never heard from them again," Susan says.

Tom finally swigs from his can and drains what remains. He rises to his feet. "Probably weren't cut out for country life is all. Rude to leave like they did. Beers in the fridge?" he asks.

I nod and he retrieves a fresh can, opening it as he goes. I'm barely halfway through mine. Priya is tense. I feel her stiffen at the revelation. Her hand finds mine and she squeezes it. I think it's a sign we bring things around to the point.

"So," I say, trying to line my thoughts up clearly and concisely, ready to relay them to my aunt and cousin. "So, we were browsing the old holiday let reviews for a bit of fun, curious to see what people thought of the area and the cottage and so forth. We couldn't help but notice the sites suggest the cottage is undergoing renovations but will be available again soon. We figured it was just a mistake, but best to let you know."

Susan sips from her glass, her eyes down as if checking her drink for rogue flies. Tom grunts.

"Knew we should've changed that," he mutters before taking a big gulp from his Budweiser.

"Shut up," Aunt Susan hisses. Despite his size and bulk, Tom shrinks before his mother's icy tone.

"I thought we could stay as long as we wanted to?" Priya asks, shifting forward in her seat. The fire shines upon the left side of her face. In its glow, she is beautiful, she is deadly.

"Well, we've been hard up, you see. Times are tough," Susan says, staring into the fire.

"So, you fancied a free refurb, did you?" Priya says. She sits forwards now, aiming the full force of her rage at Susan and Tom.

"It's not what you think," Tom says, though offers nothing further, suggesting it's precisely what we think.

The thumping noise picks up again. Is it the house? Is something wrong with the house?

Susan stands and Tom follows suit, draining the rest of his can first.

"We need the place back in the new year. You can stay until then," Susan says, turning to leave.

"Hang on," Priya says, volume increasing. She stands, too. "You owe us thousands of pounds. We've put money into this place on the promise it's ours for as long as we want it. Tom's your nephew, your family!"

Susan stops in the doorway. "Got a contract?" she says simply.

I can't quite believe my ears. After everything – and Susan is fully aware of our pain – this is happening, Aunt Susan is scamming us. Tom, too. We were close, once. Maybe that was a lie as well.

Priya and I stand there, both at a loss for words.

"Thought not," Susan says. "Tom, come on."

Tom opens the door, and they leave.

I turn to Priya. There are tears in her eyes. They're forming in mine, too. She throws herself into my arms, her floral perfume clouding my raucous mind, and sobs.

HOUSE

You see they are upset, and they entwine into each other. You feel protective of them and, at the same time, sense an opportunity to prove how much you care for them. But interference has proven problematic so far. Do you risk one last attempt to help? From the conversation with the caretaker and her son, it seems they cannot stay with you unless you do something anyway. Do something: risk losing them. Do nothing: lose them.

You create a diversion. The kitchen taps bursts, spurting water in an arc through the air. They both run through and try to quell the leak, she by grabbing a towel to swallow the water, he by diving under the sink to find the source of the problem. Good. You see they are distracted.

You turn your attention to the caretaker and her son. For too long, their neglect shaped you, tarnished you, ruined you. No longer.

They are walking to their car. It is parked out on the gravel, but sufficient distance from the other car. You wait until they enter the vehicle. She walks slowly. He treads heavily. Finally, he slams shut his car door and they are both inside. You start the ground trembling, focusing the movement to the area beneath the caretaker's car. You hear their questions, their confusion, but they stay seated. They scream at the first crack. The back wheels of the car dip as the ground opens up. The car tilts at an angle, and they are shouting now, screaming even. They go for the doors, but you are too fast. You have the earth rise up to block each door, two great spikes stopping the vehicle's occupants from leaving. They are starting to realise it is a cage. You refocus on the cracks in the ground. You widen them, tearing open the gravel driveway as if with giant hands. The car tumbles further. Its sides and windows scratch along the rough and rugged walls of the sinkhole you're creating. The screaming continues, but you are too far along to stop. Not that you want to stop. They deserve this. They want to take your new family away from you. You won't allow that. You wait until the car submerges fully beneath the ground, gravel and rocky debris raining down upon the windscreen. And, just as those giant hands pried apart the earth, so too can they clap it back together. The car splinters and shatters. It leaks fluids and squeezes into some grotesque and flat shape. So, too, the caretaker and her son. Juices leak from orifices, organs burst, bones are ground down. Flesh flattens and minces into the finest pieces. They scream no more. Their blood seeps into the earth. You can taste it.

The sinkhole recedes until there are no visible cracks left, no scars upon the area. Gravel covers the driveway as it always has. Stars twinkle in the sky. The moon stares down upon a peaceful cottage. You are satisfied with your work. You hope they are, too.

PRIYA

THE TAP STOPS SPOUTING water abruptly. I toss the soaking wet towel aside and step away while Simon ducks out from beneath the sink. Strange. Two minutes of mayhem and done? I can't tell if I'm over-sensitive to the idea the house is manipulating everything or if I'm right to be, but this strikes me as unusual timing. We've effectively being kicked out of the house. Sure, we have a couple more months, but that's it. Maybe the house is unhappy. Maybe this is how a house cries.

"Let's get to bed. We can clean up in the morning. I've got to take a look in the loft space anyway. Think there's a roof leak above the bedroom," Simon says. He holds out his hand and I take it. A half-empty bottle of wine sits on the coffee table, along with empty glasses and beer cans.

"It's like being students again," I muse, trying to distract from thoughts of our situation.

We reach the bedroom, and Simon pulls me into a hug. "I'm so sorry," he whispers into my ear. "I never thought for a second they could be so callous."

I squeeze him back. "We'll work something out. I have friends who are solicitors. There must be some legal recourse for us to pursue."

He nods and breathes into my neck. He must be exhausted. But then he pulls round to my front and kisses me with a burning passion we've been missing since, well, for a long time. I kiss him back. He pulls his jumper and t-shirt over his head. I unbutton my shirt and let it slide to the floor. I hear the pitter-patter of rain against the roof and window, a spray, as if a storm whips up from nowhere. I reach to unhook my bra and pause. Simon, halfway through pulling his jeans off, notices.

"Something wrong?" he asks.

"It's just...the house," I reply.

He looks crestfallen. It's been a long time since we were intimate. I hate to disappoint him, but this suddenly feels, and I have no better word for it, icky. There is nowhere private when the walls are eyes.

Simon nods. "This fucking house."

SIMON

NEITHER OF US SLEEPS well. Priya is at her laptop in the lounge, fire blazing, coffee in hand. She's planning to contact a couple of friends to outline our situation, but I'm not confident we're going to get anywhere. I don't object to Priya trying though. Her anger needs funnelling somewhere.

I have the ladder leaning against the bedroom wall. The stain in the corner of the ceiling looks even bigger, somehow. A part of me thinks to hell with it, I'm not likely to be here much longer and it's not my problem. But another part of me is curious. Strange noises. Now this stain expanding when, considering the work the roofer's put in, it should be receding.

I slip a torch into my hoodie front pocket and climb the ladder. The small loft space entrance is a flimsy bit of MDF sitting over the hole. It's just wide enough that I'll squeeze through. Already, before pushing it open, there's a damp odour hovering here, like you might get from a pile of dirty leaves after a heavy rain.

I push the thin lid in. Immediately, three things assail me. Unseasonable warmth, sheer darkness, and a rotten smell. Maybe a squirrel really is up here and dead.

I pull the torch from my pocket, flick it on, climb to the top of the ladder, and poke my head through the gap. The stench is nearly overwhelming. I place my hand inside the loft for balance and it touches something wet and sticky, gluey even. I shine the torch at my hand and it's as pink as Pepto Bismol. I shudder. I raise my hand to my nose and, yep, that's the smell alright. And the stuff isn't cold to touch like most liquids: it's warm.

I roll the torchlight around me. There's rope everywhere. Hang on. Is that rope? They're glistening and pinkish, too. And they're pulsating. Everywhere I flash the torch is a strange web of thick stringy stuff that seems to disappear through crevices and into the walls of the house. Then there's that thumping sound. Louder and clearer up here. It starts up and keeps going.

Thump. Thump. Thump.

I point the torch to where the noise sounds from and, as it finds the source, I need to suppress a huge wave of nausea. An enormous fleshy sac is baked into the far corner. Some gelatinous substance covers it; the pink stuff I stuck my hand into. The rope-like things all run from this horrifying sac, a sac which pulses, no, beats. The bottom half of it is banging into the floorboards.

Thump. Thump. Thump.

Things begin to make sense. At least, in the context of this house. When we hear the thumping, the beats are accelerating, harder, effusive. This monstrosity, for I can't think of a more apt word, is something altogether alive. Meaning Priya is right. About everything. And this? This is the heart of the home.

The viscous liquid seeps forth and pools near the entrance to the loft space. Is there a wound to the heart? Is this staining a by-product of its slow death? I don't know. I don't know how to communicate with the house. If I did, would I want to? Evidently, it has the ability to trap us here, to hold us against our will. So why hasn't it so far? Perhaps…it's trying to help? Acceleration in heart rate might be anxiety or nerves or fear. Ghost Lily to keep me happy, maybe? Oh! What a fool I am.

It knows I'm here, surely?

And then I see the ropey things shoot forwards, wrap around my arms. They tighten and the torch slips from my grasp. They yank me through the hole and into the loft space.

PRIYA

THE BITTERNESS OF BLACK coffee reminds me of our honeymoon in Rome. Can we get the good times back? Somehow, our experiences at the cottage continue to strengthen a bond I'd thought broken. I have hope now.

I click send on an email to a couple of solicitor friends regarding Susan's double-cross, for that is what she's done, in effect. I don't even want to stay here, but it's the principle of the matter. She's got herself a free refurb by lying to her nephew. You see stories like this on daytime telly, but you never think you'll be in one. You never think you'll be in a haunted house story either, but we are, of a sort. But there's nothing dead here. Quite the opposite.

"This house isn't haunted," I whisper to myself. Then it occurs to me: but we are.

Notepad flashes up on my laptop screen. I didn't open it.

The cursor dances across the screen.

HE HAS FOUND ME. I AM SCARED.

Found me? Who? Wait, does it mean Simon? Oh no. I don't want to risk the house doing something rash.

What can I do?

I stare at the cursor. I haven't heard anything since Simon put the ladder up, and he's only one room over, but I daren't move from the screen, daren't shift from this line of communication. The house is reaching out for a reason.

IS HE TRYING TO HURT ME? I AM ALREADY HURT.

Already hurt? How can a house be hurt? I suppose it's alive, so maybe it can die?

He doesn't want to hurt you. We can help. What's happening?

I can feel my heart as a battering ram against the inside of my ribcage. My face flushes with heat with every message.

COME TO US.

I push the laptop aside and rush through to the bedroom. The ladder stands there, ascending into the open loft space, but Simon is nowhere to be seen. A single slipper lies on the floor by the foot of the ladder. A torch, still turned on, is beside it. And there's a blotchy stain on the carpet. Pink drips of something litter the ladder rungs. Oh my, the stain on the ceiling is growing almost before my eyes. Half the ceiling is dark. It resembles an eclipse, the light eaten away slowly, gradually, inevitably. And the smell. Wow. Rotten eggs, but worse.

I pick up the torch and take tentative steps up the ladder, stopping just before my head breaches the loft space entrance. It's not a smell, it's a stench. Tears are in my eyes. I set my hands on the course wooden panels above me and raise myself above the threshold. Darkness. I see vague outlines of things but can't tell what they are. I bring the torch up and shine it towards the far corner.

I can't hold in the scream.

Simon is strung up by a web of slender limbs. One wiggles around his face, gagging him, his face seemingly bloated. His arms and legs have ribbons wrapping round them again and again, the slender limbs slithering around him like snakes. Behind him, some thick, bulbous mound of flesh threatens to spill forth and flood the loft space, flood the house. I need to do something.

"Please, stop. You're killing him!" I cry.

The writhing seems to slow up, somewhat, and Simon's mouth becomes free. He gasps for air despite the thick stench.

"Let him go. We won't hurt you. We want to look after you." I flash the torch along the open floorboards. They're slick with whatever is leaking from that thing. It has an injury. Maybe it's dying, even.

I climb fully into the loft space, but the stringy appendages squeeze again and Simon screams. The sound cuts into me, a pain pure and visceral. I stop. Please, no. I can't lose him. I can't lose someone else I love.

"No, please! I can't help you on my own. I need him. You need him." I shine the torch at different spots, trying to find a mouth or eyes or something recognisable to speak at. But it's just a blob. A pulsating blob of, I don't know, cartilage and tendons and muscle.

It hesitates. It's entire sprawling form which, as I run the torchlight around the loft space, spreads in all directions and disappears into other areas of the cottage. But each tendril, each appendage, is still.

Until.

Simons rolls to my feet. I drop the torch and scoop him into my arms. He's wet and sticky, but it doesn't matter. He's gasping for breath, but at least he's still breathing. I pull him back towards the entrance but hear the wet whipcrack of a limb and look back to where the thing is, where It hides in darkness.

"We can speak through the computer. Same as before. Please, let me get Simon downstairs."

I wait a few seconds and there's no obvious attempt to impede me, so I start moving again. I help Simon onto the ladder, his breath coming back to him somewhat, and follow him down. We make it to the sofa and the fire sparks up, causing us both to jump. The house wants to help, still, but it's incapable of really interpreting what we want and need, just as we find it difficult to interpret what it wants and needs. It's so childlike in that way.

I fetch Simon a glass of water and throw a blanket over him. Pink slime covers him and, well, he stinks, but he smiles and nods at me, then sips his drink.

I grab the laptop. The house has written something in Notepad.

I AM DYING, I THINK. WILL YOU STAY WITH ME?

I feel, despite everything, a strange knot in my throat. I don't think I can refuse. Before I can type back, Simon places his cold hand on mine. He's nodding.

"Let's stay. If you want to, that is," he says.

I squeeze his hand and then let it go.

We will stay with you. Can we fix you?

Simon and I await the answer. It comes quickly.

NO. THE END WILL BE SOON. THE HOUSE WILL JUST BE A HOUSE. I HOPE YOU ARE HAPPY HERE.

A tear slides from my eye and Simon, too, is welling up, though he's doing his gruff and manly best to suppress it. The silly sod. It feels strange to think of the awful things we're still going through with this house, but we finally have some vague understanding of each other. Maybe this can be our home, after all.

HOUSE

YOU UNDERSTAND NOW THAT the strange thing you're feeling is a mortal wound. You do not know quite how it came to be this way, but just as you see humans grow old and wither, perhaps, so too do you.

And they, your friends, understand that you will be gone soon. They have given you great comfort as your life comes to an end. In particular, it is nice to know this thing you are, or rather this thing you inhabit, will go on, will continue to be warm and comfortable and free. You always thought you would be a good home for children. Maybe that can happen in the future. You're sad you will miss it, but happy it can still happen.

They are comfortable in you now. Whether the knowledge you'll soon depart causes this, or the under-standing you all came to aids it, you are pleased. You see them together in the intimate way a man and wife can be. Though you try to allow them privacy as best you possibly can.

You are happy to not cause them too much trouble anymore. You watch as men in uniforms and flashing cars arrive. A man and woman in normal clothes enter the house and talk to your friends for a long time. It seems to be about the caretaker and her son, but your friends know nothing about their disappearance and haven't seen them for a while. You worry you will need to do something about these visitors, but the conversation comes and goes with little consequence and, eventually, they leave. Your friends say nothing to you about it, so things must be okay. You do not wish to cause them more trouble.

It's not long after the strangers visit that you feel yourself failing. The sensation, your command of your extremities, dulls and recedes. You no longer control this whole plot, you lose the array of abilities you once had. With a last flush of strength and will, you send them a message.

THANK YOU

SIMON

PRIYA AND I ARE sitting in the lounge with the fire blazing when, without there being any draught or force acting upon it, the flames disappear as if an invisible mouth swallows them whole.

We stare at each other a moment. Priya throws a hand to her mouth.

I jump up and run through to the bedroom, near enough skidding to a stop on the thick carpet. I gasp. Seconds later, Priya is at my shoulder.

"Oh no," she whispers.

I bring her into an embrace and we both stare at the ceiling. Where once there had been a small but growing stain in one corner, there now is only stain. The entire ceiling is several shades darker. Something wet is seeping into it. The smell ripens by the second of putrefying flesh, of death.

"Do you want to check the loft space?" Priya asks.

I shake my head, no. "Whatever is up there now, it's dead. We'll have to sleep at Susan's bungalow in town for a few nights while we organise a deep clean here."

Priya presses her face into my chest. I run my fingers through her hair.

"Lucky we can do that," she mutters.

Since Susan and Tom's disappearance, and with the help of Priya's solicitor connections, we successfully applied for guardianship of their properties. They can't be legally declared dead for seven years but, after some quiet discussions, we concluded it is highly unlikely they'll be turning back up again. Priya and I pack some clothes and toiletries and grab a few electronics before heading out to the car. A thick, cold mist covers the moors like a blanket. We can't even see the trees across the way. The blanket descends upon the house, cloaking its corpse in a lugubrious manner. We stand together on the gravel of the driveway and glance at our home. We'll make it the best home it can possibly be. We'll make it something Lily would have loved. We'll make it something another child will love.

Priya slips her hand into mine and looks up at me, browns eyes glistening like marbles. I kiss her softly on the lips. Things will never be the same but, somehow, someway, there's meaning in our lives again and, with it, comes hope.

We get into the car and drive away. There's a lot for us to do.

Acknowledgements

Firstly, I'd like to thank my editor and publisher, Ariell Cacciola, for taking a chance on my strange little haunted house tale. And, also, for including it in something like the Northern Weird Project, of which I'm immensely proud to be involved in.

A shout out to Luísa Dias for the wonderful cover - real artists are irreplaceable.

Additionally, I'd like to offer thanks to anyone who's ever published my work. Chief among those is Ashley Hutchison at Lost Boys Press, whose repeated championing of my short stories was a great confidence boost when it was sorely needed.

A huge thank you to my friends and family, whose pockets remain lighter and bookshelves heavier because of their support for my work. And thanks to all the friends I've found through writing, especially my Writing Commisery comrades. I know I'm one of the lucky ones.

To my mum and sisters, your support is keenly felt. To my dad, I wish you were here to see this.

And, finally, to my wife, Rachel, and our beautiful daughter, Flo. You've already made my life a success. The books are just a bonus.

About the Author

Stephen Howard (he/him) is an English novelist and short story writer from Manchester, now living in Cheshire with his wife, Rachel, and their daughter, Flo. An English Literature and Creative Writing graduate from the Open University, his work has been published by Lost Boys Press, The No Sleep Podcast, Metastellar, and others. He's also published one novel, a comic fantasy titled *Beyond Misty Mountain*, and the collections *Condemned To Be, Little Book of Horrors*, and *Ophelia in the Underworld and Other Melancholy Tales* (Alien Buddha Press, 2023).

About The Northern Weird Project

This book is a part of The Northern Weird Project
by Wild Hunt Books, a collection of six pocket-sized
novellas by authors who are writing and living in the
North of England.

Incorporating eerie and uncanny incidents, these
novellas investigate aspects of the North through set-
ting, subject and character.

All books in this series are available to order from our
bookshop.
https://www.wildhuntbooks.co.uk/bookshop

More From The Northern Weird Project

(Don't) Call Mum
by Matt Wesolowski

Leo is just trying to catch his train back home to the village of Malacstone in North East England. But there's disorder at the station, and when a loud young man heading for London boards the train accidentally, a usually easy journey descends into darkness and chaos. The train soon breaks down in the middle of nowhere, and as night falls, something...or *someone* steps out of the distance. Is it a man or something far more sinister?

The Off-Season
by Jodie Robins

It's the off-season in the seaside resort town of Blackpool, where Tommy never imagined he would return. His relationship has broken down, so he returns home to keep an eye on his widowed father. While counting down the hours before attending the funeral of a well-loved friend, a mysterious group turns up on the seafront. One by one, the locals are entranced by their presence until Tommy and his father can no longer resist the allure. Tommy soon discovers a secret desire his father has been harbouring for his entire life.

The Retreat
by Gemma Fairclough

Richard's sister Julie returns home from a mysterious wellness facility in remote Cumbria in 1994. He's convinced that this place was a cult and was the cause of his sister's eventual suicide. Finally, after years as an unaccomplished academic, he decides to investigate the disturbing accusations against the Hartman Retreat Centre. Then he meets Lucy, a young woman whose story is eerily similar to his sister's decades before. Richard is determined to unearth what's really been happening at the Hartman Retreat Centre but more importantly, who is Charles Hartman, the celebrated healer who casts a powerful hold over all who come to the retreat.

Good Boy

by Neil McRobert

After a boy vanishes on the outskirts of a small Northern town, a woman spies from her window a mysterious man digging a grave in the exact spot of the disappearance. However, when she confronts him, the man's true purpose is far more chilling than she could have imagined and the history of the town's fatal past unfolds. What has been hiding in this small northern town all these years? A gripping story of supernatural horror, nostalgia and mystery.

Turbine 34

by Katherine Clements

It's 2035 and England is experiencing the hottest summer in living memory. Heather Sutcliffe, a 61-year-old environmental scientist, is tasked with evaluating the impact of a controversial new wind farm on the West Yorkshire moors. Camped out alone at Turbine 34 which was built on the ancient peat bog, she soon discovers signs of the devastation caused by the construction, she begins to see things that shouldn't be there. Heather has dedicated her life to protecting the moor, but will it protect her?

Wild Hunt Books would like to thank the following
Lifetime Supporters:

Daniel Sorabji
Jan Penovich
Blaise Cacciola

BECOME A SUPPORTER BY CONTACTING US AT

INFO@WILDHUNTBOOKS.CO.UK

The Publisher would also like to thank the following early supporters of The Northern Weird Project:

Aidan Smith

Alex Herod

Ali W

Alicia Lomas-Gross

Anthony Martin

Beth Baskett

Bethany Vare

Blair Rose

Carmen

Charlotte Platt

Charlotte Tierney

Emma Armshaw

Freya S

George Dunn

Heidi Marjamäki

Ianthe May

J. Aaron Courts CWO4, USMC, Retired

Jeff

Jennifer B. Lyday

K. Wicks

Kelsey Stoddard

Kirsty Logan

Laura Elliott

Lisa Elliott

Lynne G

Mandy Bublitz

Mark Taylor

Martyn Waites

Monica Voynovska

Nicola Leedham

Nina Woodcock

Rachel Bridgeman

Rosie Warfield

Samuel Best

Sheena E. Perez

Sonja Zimmermann

Sophy Holland

Stefanie Olivola

Stephanie Eleanor Henrichs Welch

Stewart Mack

Vince Fairclough